SMUGGLER'S GULCH

The dark-eyed lady wants Jake
Staggs to collect the bounties on
twenty members of an outlaw band.
She might be crazy, but the only
other option for this wanted man is
the hangman's noose. He can easily
ride into the rustlers' camp at
Smuggler's Gulch — he went there
once before. But will Kit Blanchard
allow him to leave . . . alive? Now he
must try again — for the sake of a
madwoman. Meanwhile, should Jake
fail, Marshal Trouffant waits to hang
him.

Books by Logan Winters
in the Linford Western Library:

OVERLAND STAGE
INCIDENT AT COYOTE WELLS
DARK ANGEL RIDING
ROGUE LAW
THE LAND GRABBERS
THE LEGACY

LOGAN WINTERS

SMUGGLER'S GULCH

Complete and Unabridged

LINFORD
Leicester

First published in Great Britain in 2010 by
Robert Hale Limited
London

First Linford Edition
published 2011
by arrangement with
Robert Hale Limited
London

British Library CIP Data

Winters, Logan.
  Smuggler's gulch. - -
  (Linford western library)
  1. Bounty hunters- -Fiction. 2. Outlaws- -
  Fiction. 3. Western stories. 4. Large type books.
  I. Title II. Series
  823.9'2–dc22

  ISBN 978–1–4448–0764–6

Published by
F. A. Thorpe (Publishing)
Anstey, Leicestershire

Set by Words & Graphics Ltd.
Anstey, Leicestershire
Printed and bound in Great Britain by
T. J. International Ltd., Padstow, Cornwall

1

It wasn't the kind of place you were likely to run across except by chance. There weren't many maps of this corner of Arizona Territory, and few of them were more than guesses sketched out by surveyors who wished to get out as soon as possible and leave the broken, arid land to those who deserved it: the rattlesnakes and Yavapai Indians, who were not warlike, but a gloomy people, possibly a result of living a life mostly devoted to searching for water and food on this hard-bitten land.

Jacob Staggs, mostly referred to as 'Jake', stumbled upon the canyon in that way — by chance. He had been crossing the long white sand low desert and took the risk of riding his broken down, weary buckskin horse into the rocky highlands when they presented themselves. At the very least, he figured, rising another few thousand feet must lead him to a cooler place to die.

Jacob 'call me Jake' Staggs was on the near side of twenty-five years of age and had nothing to show for that spent quarter of a century as yet. Motherless, fatherless, he had watched his uncle killed in a border skirmish and had begun wandering. In Mexico they had threatened to hang him for the crime of killing a local man's burro. The fact that the man riding the burro had a ten-gauge shotgun aimed in Jake's direction at the time did not sway the authorities. Jake's shot had struck the burro and killed it. He was a stranger in a strange land and no friendly ears were willing to listen to his side of the story. The only thing to do was to run and he had. The buckskin horse he now rode had been taken from the American cattleman who had talked him into riding to Mexico in the first place. The man's name was Bert Stiles, and it was he who had persuaded Jake to join his cattle drive and then proceeded to stiff Jake and the entire crew on their wages, leaving them broke and far from home at the end of the trail.

That was the extent of Jake's crime spree, but he was an outlaw now on either side of the border, he supposed. And a damned unsuccessful one at that. The soles of his boots were showing holes — a sure indicator of a man in dire straits in this part of the country where a man's boots were expected to last longer than his pony, the boots being the less used: a man desperate enough to walk from one side of the street to a saloon on the opposite side showed himself to be no real cowboy.

Jake Staggs was also out of water, and that troubled him much more than the idea that someone might see his worn out boots. He rode higher into the hills, which showed no vegetation besides an occasional yucca and scattered patches of cholla cactus, only endless stacks of yellow-gray boulders jumbled together in a sort of devil's playground. He could feel the buckskin stumble from time to time and he stroked its neck in sympathy but that was all he could do to relieve the weary animal as it strove to pick a path upward through the weather-scoured boulders.

The furnace winds of the desert that Jake had hoped to escape blew more fiercely as they climbed. The desert wind snatched at his faded blue shirt and at the horse's mane and tail, as if unseen fingers were trying to offer a warning and turn him back from his intended path. Maybe a man should pay attention to such small omens.

There being nothing behind him but the bluish heat-blurred vista of the long desert, Jake rode doggedly on throughout the stupor-inducing day.

When he found the canyon his reaction was that of a man stumbling through a mirage believing he has found an oasis yet uncertain as to its reality.

Cresting yet another boulder-strewn ridge, Jake felt a cool updraft; at the same time his horse's ears pricked and its nostrils flared in eager anticipation: the horse smelled water. Jake's senses weren't that refined, but he could see green, living things. A staggered row of shaggy Mexican fan palm trees made its way up toward a feeder canyon, indicating water. A few yards on, he saw the gorge itself. Scattered live oak trees grew there and a clump of cottonwood trees showed the silver of the underleaves as they shifted in the dry breeze.

It was difficult to hold the buckskin back now that he smelled water and simultaneously heard the nickering of others of its kind. Now visible to Jake in a roughly made pen, they were standing near a stone house which was squat, undistinguished, weathered and yet so solid that it appeared to be almost a part of the rugged hills surrounding it.

'Steady,' Jake said to the horse, leaning forward to study the layout. It was certainly no settlement he was now looking at. Far from any stage line, and other convenience, it really had no reason to exist. Certainly it was not a cattle ranch or a horse ranch, although there seemed to be a significant number of horses in the pen, twenty or thirty at least. The graze he could see from the boulder-cluttered hillside was sparse and brown. There could be no farther pasture, the place being tucked tightly inside the folded rocky hills. What, then, was it? Who would wish to remain long in this isolated desert canyon for any reason whatever?

The buckskin horse was trembling beneath him, out of exhaustion and mingled excitement. Jake's tongue clove to his palate. His lips were split, and his face blistered from the long ride over the barren desert. He made up his mind: there really was no choice.

There was water in the canyon; he was going down.

The horse impatiently wound its way downslope, following a switchback trail through the boulders, some of which were stacked more than fifty feet high, all of which radiated the heat of the day and cut off every whisper of the cooling breeze. The ride seemed a descent into hell. One more omen that Jake should perhaps have heeded.

They finally reached the flats of the long, narrow valley, and Jake moved the buckskin forward across grass so dry that it crackled beneath the horse's hoofs as they passed. There was a cluster of dusty-leafed live oak trees beside the trail leading toward the house he had seen, and now a woman burst suddenly from them.

She wore a striped skirt and a ruffled white blouse. Her dark hair was in a tangle as she rushed toward Jake, her hands upraised.

'Save me, oh save me!' she cried as she reached Jake's halted horse. He stared in bewilderment as the woman, slender, somewhere around the age of twenty-five, caught the buckskin's bridle in one hand, touched his knee with the other and lifted pleading eyes to him. 'Thank God someone's come at last to deliver me from this hell!' she screamed frantically and then, as Jake watched, stunned, the sheer panic that had contorted her face fell away and was replaced by wide-eyed glee. She began to laugh loud and long, placing one hand to her breast. Her head rocked from side to side with amusement. A man emerged from the oak grove and looked the woman up and down, studied Jake Staggs and said:

'This is our Sarah. She's quite mad, you know. Go on back to the house, Sarah. Do you have to frighten every stranger that passes through like that?'

'I'm sorry, Worthy,' the woman, Sarah, said, keeping her eyes down. She traced arcs in the sandy soil with the toe of her small scuffed boot. With one last amused glance at Jake Staggs, she hoisted her skirts and ran away spryly toward the stone house. The man called Worthy looked at Jake and his well-used horse and said:

'You must be wishing for water. There's a well ahead, but easier for your pony to drink from the little rill beyond the palm trees.'

The man was stocky, stubby almost. He had pouched eyes and a small nose that seemed to be retreating from his face to make room for his expanding jowls. But he wore a smile as well as a low-slung six-gun.

'The girl . . . ?' Jake began, but Worthy shrugged the question off saying:

'If you knew our Sarah, you wouldn't pay any attention to that. She's not quite right. It comes and goes. Mostly she's good company, and a fair cook.'

Knowing nothing of matters and not needing to, Jake walked his horse forward in the direction indicated and soon came upon the rill which tumbled down from some high artesian spring, passed among the stacks of yellow boulders and spread itself to feed the struggling trees and scant grass.

It was much cooler near the water in the shade of not only the shaggy swaying palm trees but the shifting

9

cottonwoods. Jake watched the buck-skin carefully, not wanting it to drink too much of the cold, crystal clear water, yet he himself had to take care not to make the same mistake. There is nothing more vital to life than water, and nothing that can satisfy the body long deprived of it but water. Finally, as the buckskin lifted its nose from the rill once again, dripping water from its muzzle which the high sun caught and silvered, Jake backed the reluctant horse away from the stream into the shade of the cottonwood trees, which were just beginning to bud out with the fuzzy white seedpods which gave them their name.

Jake sat with his back against one of the trees, watching the enclosed valley where still there was little movement — no working men, no riders. No one called across the yard. He had, as yet, only seen Sarah and the stubby little man, Worthy, but judging by the number of horses in the pen there must be others around. Jake considered all of the possibilities and the thought occurred to him that this might be a place where men who do not wish to be found could live. The horses, perhaps, were meant to be traded to men like himself: men on the run. He wondered if he had not wandered into some sort of robbers' roost, but it was only idle speculation and since he planned on traveling on as soon as the buckskin was in decent shape again, it was really a matter of indifference to him.

There was a subject which concerned him and continued to grow in importance. Passing the house earlier he had tasted the scent of cooking on the air. Roast beef, for sure, and what might have been freshly baked bread. His stomach, minutes ago satisfied with the water, now began to complain and demand more solid nourishment.

Well, Jake thought as he collected the reins of the buckskin and started to lead it toward the house, Worthy had said that Sarah, mad as she might be, was a good cook. Maybe they would let Jake try his luck at their table. His pockets were empty, he knew; Bert Stiles, damn his eyes, had left the entire crew of drovers broke and stranded in Mexico without so much as a nickel or a promise.

Maybe Worthy would be willing to stand a single meal for a wandering man. Hopefully, Jake Staggs wandered toward the house.

Passing the rough corral where the horses craned their necks to get a look at his buckskin, Jake saw the squat Worthy standing on the wooden porch in front of the stone house. He was not smiling, but neither was there apparent dislike on his face.

'Hungry, are you?' Worthy asked with a nod. 'I figured you'd be along. Come on in and have a seat. Panda will take care of your horse.' Who Panda might have been, Jake did not know. He had seen no one else in the yard, and nothing moving but the leaves in the trees and light blow sand the wind picked up in its passing. Worthy suggested:

'Don't say anything to Sarah about before — she's likely already forgotten about your meeting by now, the way her mind is.'

'What made her the way she is?' Jake asked. Worthy frowned and looked around at the rising rocky hills and at the white sun in a white sky and shook his head.

'The desert, I guess,' he said softly. 'It gets to some people after a while, you know. I've met old prospectors, desert rats loonier than anyone they ever had in Bedlam.' He shrugged, 'But they don't bother anyone wandering the desert by themselves, do they?'

'So Sarah wants someone to rescue her from the desert?' Jake asked as he looped the buckskin's reins to the rough hitching post and stepped up onto the porch.

'What she wants to be rescued from is something that exists only in her own mind,' Worthy said with a heavy shake of the head. 'Maybe only from herself. But enough of that; let's sit down and eat, shall we?'

The room was small, but planks had been laid down for flooring. Food was already on the table — a rolled roast beef large enough to feed a dozen men, freshly baked bread, hominy and yams. Sarah was there as well.

There was a small kitchen area off to one side and beside it a short corridor running toward the back rooms of the stone house. Sarah could be seen from time to time, flitting about. From the shadows where she stood Jake saw her smiling broadly one minute, frowning and shaking her head the next. She jabbed her finger vigorously at herself and then at Jake, then at the ceiling overhead. She was alternately ghostly, cheerful and pleading. It wasn't clear if Worthy saw any of this; if so he gave no indication. The bulky little man continued to eat with his head hung over his plate.

The meal, plain as it was, was immensely satisfying. The afternoon steadily cooled, and as Jake Staggs stepped out onto the porch he took the time to stretch, loosen his belt and deeply breathe in the fresh air. He felt a whole man again. He could not see his buckskin horse, but for the moment he did not feel concerned. Worthy stepped out behind him, the swaying porch giving under his heavy tread. Lighting a pipe, he stood beside Jake in studied silence.

'This isn't a bad little set-up you've got here,' Jake said to the stubby little man, 'though I can't say it's the sort of life I'd want.'

'Not many are suited for it,' Worthy answered. 'I think it's the silence of the place that gets to most people.'

'That could be,' Jake answered. He could hear a covey of desert quail somewhere along the creek, but for the rest there was only silence. 'Anyway, I thank you for saving me and letting me sit down to your table.'

'Meaning you'll be traveling on?' Worthy asked, puffing vigorously at his pipe.

'As soon as possible,' Jake said. 'No offense, but there's nothing much here for a man, is there?'

'Not much,' Worthy agreed. 'Not much at all.' He looked briefly toward the pale sky and then let his gaze meet Jake's. 'Are you on the run?'

'What makes you ask that?' Jake asked, stumbling over his tongue. Worthy smiled and shook his head.

'Nothing. I don't mean to pry, but we don't get many men riding through here unless they're trying to get away from something or somebody.'

Jake frowned. He did not answer. He did not know if he was on the run or not, not exactly. Would the Mexican authorities mount a manhunt for him across the border over the killing of a donkey? He doubted it. Or would Bert Stiles be angry enough over the loss of the buckskin to pursue Jake across the long desert? That seemed just as unlikely. Jake decided that no, he was not running away from anything. Perhaps he was just desperately searching for some place to run *to*.

It made no difference. This isolated dry canyon was not what he was looking for and he only repeated, 'I'll be hitting the road as soon as my horse is ready to travel.'

'Good enough,' Worthy said, tapping his dead pipe on the hitchrail to knock the dottle free. 'You probably would like to get a little rest first.' He inclined his head toward a ramshackle stone and pole structure not far away through the cotton-woods. 'The barn's over there. You can curl up until the day cools. I'll show you the way to Yuma, if that's where you're heading.'

Jake had no idea where he was heading. Yuma might be all right. He might find something there to do, something to care about.

'Get your rest,' Worthy said encouragingly. 'There's no one around except for Panda, and he won't bother you. He likely won't even talk to you if you do happen to see him, but pay him no mind, he's only a sad, regretful old Indian. Panda is on the run too, from his own people. He once made the mistake of scalping a few men who did not deserve it.'

Not exactly words of comfort for a man intending to sleep in a strange place, but Jake's weariness could be stayed no further. He ambled across the ranch yard to the nearby barn and slipped in after searching with his eyes for the mysterious and mostly invisible Panda, but the Yavapai didn't seem to be lurking nearby.

Panda, it seemed, had taken good care of the buckskin horse, for Jake found it standing in one of the dark stalls munching at fresh alfalfa hay. Where the hay could have come from Jake couldn't guess, but it figured that they would need a lot of hay with all the horses standing in the corral. In passing, Jake had looked the horses over. They were good stock, each and every one of them, of all hues from a burnished roan, its hide glistening in the sun, to a small dun with thickly bunched chest muscles. They wore mixed brands, most of them unfamiliar to Jake, though he did spot two of them wearing the Anchor brand. He had ridden with a man named Pete Storey while with Bert Stiles, and Pete, who was out of Flagstaff in the high country of central Arizona, said that he had ridden for Anchor which was a fair-sized outfit.

The question that presented itself, of course, was what this grass poor ranch tucked away in the barren desert needed with so many horses. Jake still had not seen another person around save the three he had been introduced to — if it was possible to say he had been introduced to Panda.

No matter. There is a time for thinking and a time for sleeping, and the heaviness of Jake's eyelids told him which time had now arrived. He loosened up a pile of hay in the shadowed corner of the barn and lay down, hat over his eyes. When the day cooled and the buckskin had rested, he would be on his way again. Yuma, he

19

guessed, could not be that bad a town to start over. He yawned as he made that decision, crossed his arms over his chest and fell off to sleep.

It was still warm when Jake awoke a few hours later, the barn having held the heat of the day, but outside the sky was beginning to color — rose pink and deep violet — and he could hear the frogs beginning to give voice to their night complaints up along the rill. If he left now he could make Yuma by midnight, he believed.

Rising stiffly, he stretched and walked to the buckskin which seemed happy to see him but carried a worried gleam in its eyes as if knowing that this human would soon take him away from the comfort of the barn and force him again to make his way across the endless desert. Jake stroked the horse's muzzle and looked around until he found his saddle slung over a partition, his bridle hanging on a rusty bent nail on a nearby post.

There was a blur of motion in the

opposite corner of the barn and he saw a dark figure scuttle from the gloomy dimness into the half-bright dusk. He hadn't had a good look at him, but the man was an Indian, that was for sure. Panda, it seemed, did not care for any sort of human contact. It made no difference to Jake. He was feeling rested, fed and ready to ride.

Smoothing his striped saddle blanket on the buckskin's back, he saddled the horse, slipped it its bit and led it outside where the multi-colored sky lined the jagged ridges of the surrounding peaks and the coolness of the evening welcomed him.

He considered going by the rock house and saying thanks and so long to Worthy, but there seemed little point in it. He did glance that way and by the dull light of a lantern within saw the strangely pathetic figure of a woman, a shawl across her head and shoulders, her mouth open as if pleading, her fingers spread against the bluish pane of glass.

'Sorry, Sarah,' he muttered, keeping his eyes turned down. 'I'm not the one you are waiting for.'

Before he had hit leather again he came upon Worthy standing in the center of the dry-grass yard, hands on his hips, staring northward. Jake started to speak, but Worthy held up a silencing hand. In a few minutes Jake, too, became aware of it: someone was approaching. There was dust drifting on the wind and the sound of hoofbeats — many of them. Standing beside Worthy he waited, watching in puzzlement.

In another minute two riders rode toward them at speed, swung down from their lathered ponies and opened the corral gates, hieing the animals standing there to the far confines. Behind these two came the horses, not in a rush, but in wild-eyed surprise. A half dozen men herded them along through the sundown-lighted evening. Twenty or more horses of all descriptions were pushed toward the corral and urged into it with coiled ropes, whistles and yells.

The horses milled in confusion, lifting heavy dust into the air. The sky continued to darken. From out of this darkness two men on horseback approached. One of them held a double-twelve shotgun in his hand. They both looked trail-weary, angry and plain mean. Eyes appraised Jake from the shadows of their hatbrims.

'Who the hell's this, Worthy?' the man on the paint pony demanded, nodding at Jake.

'Passing stranger,' Worthy said — a little defensively, Jake thought. The man on the paint horse had narrow eyes, wide shoulders and a mouth that twisted nastily when he spoke. His sidekick was thick, brutish and bearded.

'How do you know who the hell he is? Worthy, I told you before . . . ' the man's voice broke off in exasperation.

'He's just riding out now, Blanchard,' Worthy explained. 'There's no trouble here.'

'Oh, there's trouble here,' the man called Blanchard contradicted. 'He's already seen enough to cause trouble, hasn't he? No,' the man astride the paint pony continued with a heavy shake of his head, 'there is trouble, unless he's a blind man. And as for riding out . . .

'You're going nowhere, stranger. Hand over your revolver and that Henry repeater you're toting. You'll be staying for a while. Quite a long while.'

2

It didn't require a stroke of brilliance to deduce what was going on at the isolated canyon ranch. Jake knew that he had stumbled upon a gang of horse thieves. What else could explain the driving of a large herd of horses onto this poor range, the thirty or so sleek ponies already penned in the yard? Jake Staggs was really not concerned about it in any way — they were not his horses, after all, and his own mount rightfully belonged to Bert Stiles. All he had wanted to do was water his buckskin and keep drifting on. Now that wasn't going to be too easy.

Kit Blanchard, the narrow-eyed man who seemed to be the leader of the gang, had ordered two of his rough-necks to take Jake by the arms and lead him to a small stone shed along the creek. He had been thrown in, the heavy door locked and he now found himself seated in the darkness with the man he knew to be Panda.

Why the Indian was also locked in he did not know, but it seemed to be something that the Yavapai was used to, for Panda sat in a corner, knees drawn up, his arms looped around them, saying nothing, his face expressing no anger or resentment.

There was a single window high on the wall, barred and far too narrow for a man to squeeze through. Through that slit, undoubtedly designed only to ventilate the close stone structure, Jake could see the last colors of the evening sky fading to darkness, dimming as were his hopes.

'What are they going to do to us?' Jake asked Panda, but the man just stared at him with opaque black eyes. Perhaps he didn't even understand English, though he must have picked up at least a few words working around the ranch. When Jake had resigned himself

to the settling darkness, the uncomfortable floor and the continued silence of
the Yavapai, the Indian's voice croaked,
like a long rusted hinge and the man
said:

'Bad days.'

Jake eagerly tried continuing the
conversation, to find out what was likely
to happen to him and if there was a way
to break out, but Panda had apparently
said all he intended to say — or all he
knew how to communicate.

The desert coolness settled; it was
remarkable how quickly the nights
could settle and how cold they became
with no atmosphere to hold the heat of
the day in. Jake began to shiver. He
seated himself as Panda had done,
drawing his knees up tightly against his
chest. For a blanket!

His teeth had begun to chatter, his
body to shiver. He could see a star or
two through the slit window, but not
enough of them to gauge the time by.
He thought it was somewhere around
ten o'clock when he heard the scraping

of boot leather against the earth and someone fumbling with the iron latch bolting the door. As it swung open, Jake tried to leap to his feet, but only succeeded in staggering away to lurch against the wall, his circulation-starved leg muscles unwilling to cooperate with his mind's commands. A huge bearded man stood outside the door, silhouetted against the star-silvered sky.

'Come on out of there,' he ordered. Jake glanced at Panda, but the Indian had not moved. It was himself that they wanted. Bending over to scoop up his hat, Jake eased out into the chill of the clear desert night.

'What's happening?' he asked the big man warily.

'They told me to get you. That's all I know.'

All Jake needed to know was that he was out of the makeshift jail and that the man in front of him was displaying a Colt revolver. He would go wherever he was to be taken without a struggle. It was back to the house, as it appeared, for they walked that way, the big man always three or four steps behind Jake, his revolver fisted tightly in his hand. The stars were strewn wildly across the black sky. The cottonwood trees and the farther line of palms stood in stark relief against them.

'Are they going to let me go?' Jake asked his oversized companion.

'They said bring you,' his escort grunted.

All right, then, Jake thought. At least they weren't going to shoot him out of hand. Maybe there was a chance to plead, argue or lie his way out of this place. They didn't want him around and he surely didn't want to stay. He assumed, rightly, that they saw him as an unwelcome witness. They couldn't have mistaken him for a lawman, could they? What sane man with a badge would have ridden alone into this armed camp?

His speculations were unimportant, he decided, as they approached the lighted stone house. They would tell him what opinion they had formed and his fate was to be decided in a few minutes on this lost and lonely canyon outpost.

Just before they mounted the sagging wooden steps and entered the house Jake saw, just for the briefest moment, the sad, huddled figure of Sarah looking at him through the lace curtains. Maybe she wasn't as mad as Worthy had said, or perhaps he had been right — this place had made her lose her mind.

They were there at the table, the last of the roast beef was nearly gone. The entire crew seemed to have eaten, but now they had drifted away. There were only four people remaining, not counting Jake and his sullen escort.

Sarah was there. Jake saw her flitting across the hallway toward a hidden room. Worthy sat at the right side of the table, looking somewhat nervous. The stubby little man's eyes shifted from point to point, never quite meeting Jake's. At the head of his table, picking his teeth, Kit Blanchard lounged recklessly, a man without a care in the world. Then there was the blonde.

She sat beside and a little behind Kit Blanchard. She wore her long blonde hair in a single braid which just then was tossed up over her shoulder as she fiddled with the ribbon tie holding it. She wore a yellowish flannel shirt with snaps instead of buttons and a pair of black jeans. She was young, blue-eyed and she smiled as she lifted those eyes to Jake Staggs. She seemed about ready to say something, but Kit Blanchard spoke first.

'That buckskin horse with the Broken T brand you're riding. It's stolen!'

Jake started to deny it, then saw no point in it. He shrugged slightly. 'I had to get away from where I was.'

'Is that the way you usually go about your business?' Kit Blanchard demanded, lowering his hand to nestle near the holstered Colt riding on his hip. Jake shook his head and told the dark-eyed man:

'I don't usually need to get away as

bad as I did this time.'

Worthy, still nervous, spoke up, 'I guess what Kit wants to know is — '

'I'll tell the man what I want to know,' Kit Blanchard said, cutting off Worthy's words. The stubby little man folded his hands together and looked away.

Kit Blanchard shifted slightly in his chair. The blonde, Jake noticed, was beaming at him as if he were her lord and master. Maybe he was. 'What I want to know,' Kit said, 'is if you would be willing to work for me. We lost a couple of good hands on the trail, and as you have seen we've got a fair-sized herd of ponies out there that have to be moved as soon as they're rested.'

'We don't have enough hay to feed them for long,' Worthy commented, daring to interrupt the leader of the band of rustlers. Blanchard didn't even glance at him.

'Look, Jake — that's your name, isn't it? — we have a lot of horses out there and the day after tomorrow we're going to have to gather them and push them down to Agua Fria. Do you know where that is?'

'I don't even know where I am,' Jake said honestly.

Kit Blanchard smiled thinly. 'Just across the border in Mexico. I've got a buyer for these horses. The thing is, we had a little trouble on the trail and we're short of men. I know you're on the run from something even if I don't know what it is. I don't care much, to tell you the truth, but you can hire on and make yourself a few dollars in the process, or we'll just keep your horse and you can start out on foot for Yuma. Of course I'm not sure you could make it; no one ever has.'

'All right,' Jake said quickly if not eagerly, 'I'm more used to herding cattle, but I'll go along with you.' He couldn't see that he had much choice. Being sent out onto the long desert on foot was the same as being sentenced to death.

'All right then,' Blanchard said with a

tight nod. 'Blanco here will show you around.' He indicated the big silent man who had escorted him to the house. 'You'll understand if we don't give you your guns back just yet.'

Blanchard rose to his feet in one easy motion, his chair scraping on the plank floor. He took the young blonde by the arm and said, 'That's settled, let's get some rest, Christi.' The woman smiled at him, turned her head once to smile at Jake as well and was led off by the arm toward the interior of the house where Sarah had long since vanished into the shadows. Worthy did not rise, in fact he had barely moved. He sat with his head hanging, heavy arms draped over the arms of the chair.

'We go now,' the big bearded Blanco said, and he nudged Jake in the ribs with the muzzle of his pistol.

'All right,' Jake said. 'You don't need that gun.'

Blanco only repeated, 'We go now,' and it was difficult for Jake to decide if Blanco was that taciturn, spoke little of the language or was just plain stupid. No matter — he was the one with the revolver, so Jake turned and led the way toward the open door into the cool desert night.

They crossed the dry grass of the yard and passed into the cottonwood grove. Fifty yards on they found a small campfire burning with men lounging around it smoking or curled up in their blankets trying to sleep. A couple of rough lean-tos had been thrown up for shelter, but there were no other structures in the outlaw camp.

'Grab a blanket and make yourself comfortable,' Blanco told him, so Jake took an Indian blanket from a pile and settled down, easing nearer to the small, wavering fire. Jake saw dark, expressionless eyes lift to study him and watched as a bottle was passed between two other men who showed no interest at all in who he might be or what he was doing there.

An older man, blond and balding with a craggy face, scooted over next to

Jake and offered his hand. 'I'm Will Sizemore. Don't pay any attention to the manners of the boys. They don't talk much, but they ride hard and shoot straight.' The flickering firelight illuminated Sizemore's lined face. Jake thought the man was a little old for this sort of work, but then he reflected, there were only two ways out for a man who hits the outlaw trail: they hang you or you get shot down.

Jake Staggs did not intend to end up that way.

'Riding south with us, are you?' Sizemore asked.

'That's what the boss says, though he's got a funny way of hiring a man on.'

Sizemore laughed dryly, 'Kit Blanchard, he takes men on any way he can. Sort of like a land pirate, he's been known to shanghai a few when we had our ranks thinned.' Sizemore lowered his voice. 'We had three men shot down this side of Tucson. The rancher who lost his horses didn't take kindly to us collecting them. We got out of there, but it was a tight spot.'

Jake asked, 'What is this place called anyway?' He indicated the width and length of the canyon with a wave of his hand. 'Has it got a name?'

'Why, this is Smuggler's Gulch,' Sizemore said with some surprise. 'You've probably heard of it, but not many men have seen it, and the law sure is never going to find it.'

Jake reflected, but no, he had never heard of the place. Apparently it loomed large in local lore, for Sizemore seemed nearly offended that Jake had never heard of the outlaw camp before. The fire burned lower. Sizemore leaned forward to add a few more sticks to the dying flames. Most of the men had rolled up in their blankets for the night by then.

'That Sarah . . . ' Jake asked hesitantly. 'What do you know about her?'

'Sarah Worthy!' Sizemore smiled and shook his head. 'The sun, the isolation, the way of life drove her over the edge a long while ago. Pretty little girl, too. It's a shame, but mister she is plain loco — anything she ever tells you, you can disbelieve it.'

'And the other woman, the blonde?'

'That's Christiana, Sarah's cousin.' Sizemore's face had lost all of its amiability. 'Don't think about her too much. She's Kit Blanchard's woman and if you look at her too long or in the wrong way, you're likely to find yourself dead.'

'I won't. Thanks for telling me.'

'I just thought you should know.' Sizemore wrapped his blanket more tightly around his shoulders and yawned. 'Anyway, there's no point in talking about women or thinking about them way out here. Wait until we hit Agua Fria and get our pay.' He chuckled, 'Then you and I can have some discussion about the Spanish women at the end of the trail.'

With that, Sizemore rolled onto his side and tugged his blanket up over his ears. Jake figured that he might as well follow suit. There was no point in sitting up even though he doubted he would be able to sleep on this night. There was no sign of Blanco. Evidently his work was done; no one had told him to stand guard over Jake. What for? Was Jake Staggs going to make a break for the rocky slopes, the desert beyond without horse, water or guns? Still, his thoughts kept him awake until very early morning. From time to time he took it upon himself to add a few sticks to the fire. The night passed in weary progression, the stars eventually dragging a wan crescent moon up from behind the rocky hills.

It was about the time that the golden sliver of the moon rose that Jake saw her in the cottonwood grove, flitting from tree to tree. She stopped once and beckoned to him before vanishing again, a slender ghost in the dark, dangerous night of Smuggler's Gulch.

3

It was crazy, riding out of Smuggler's Gulch with Sarah, but in another way it made a lot of sense. When he had risen from the low-burning campfire and slipped away from the camp into the shadowed depths of the cottonwood grove she had emerged from the darkness to rush silently to him, taking both of his hands as she looked up earnestly into his eyes.

'I've got your horse — and your guns,' she said. The moonlight shone through the upper reaches of the trees. The stars seemed to decorate the branches like Christmas baubles. Jake glanced uneasily back at the camp where the horse thieves slept.

'I've made a deal to ride with Kit,' Jake said. 'If I make a run for it now, they're liable to track me down and kill me.'

'They're liable to kill you anyway,' Sarah said, letting her hands drop away. 'You don't know Kit Blanchard like I do. Once he has no more use for you — say after you've driven the horses into Mexico — he's liable to do anything. A life means nothing to him. That's why I've got to get out of here,' she whispered fiercely.

'When I first met you — '

'I was serious at first. I had to put on my act, pretend to be crazy when Worthy showed up. I didn't know he was around.'

'But — ' Jake studied the girl closely now. There were no signs of madness, but then perhaps there would be none. At the moment she seemed to be only a frightened, desperate woman.

'You don't want to become one of them, do you?' she asked, looking toward the outlaw camp. 'A man always on the run, always being hunted.'

'No. No, I don't.'

'Then let's get moving, now! There's only an hour before sunrise, but we can slip out of the canyon before it's light. Then we ride to the nearest town. It's called Lewiston. We'll be safe there, and besides, Kit will have to have his herd on the move toward Agua Fria to sell to that Mexican bandit he deals with.'

It seemed rational but dangerous. Jake knew he had only two chances: one, to try to make his escape with Sarah, the second to fall in with the gang of horse thieves. It was an easy if not a comfortable decision to make.

'Let's get going then,' he answered at length. 'You know the way out of here, don't you?'

Sarah laughed briefly, softly. 'I know every rabbit run in this canyon. I'll get us out, for sure.' She hesitated and then added uncertainly, 'Of course, you may have to do a little fighting to get us past the sentries.'

Sentries? Well, he thought, of course there would be men watching the entrance to Smugglers Gulch with the law always on Kit Blanchard's trail. Jake didn't like the idea of fighting armed men in the darkness, but it was late, the guards would be tired of keeping watch, and their attention would be on the desert flats to the north, not on the road out. He had already made his decision; he meant to give it a try. He hesitated only because he knew that once he put his boot in the stirrup and swung aboard the saddle there was no turning back, and he was certain to face Kit Blanchard's wrath.

He sucked in a deep breath and nodded. Sarah took his hand anxiously and tugged him along toward a small copse where, indeed, the buckskin stood waiting for him alongside the sleek roan horse that he had seen earlier in the horse pen. He wondered how Sarah had managed to catch up the animals, but then she was used to the place and was probably little interfered with as she wandered around. She now wore blue jeans and a yellow shirt much the same as Christiana had worn. Perhaps it was the same shirt.

The buckskin responded with resignation as he started the horse forward, following Sarah, but it was now fed, watered and rested and he showed no balkiness other than an occasional irritated toss of its head.

They rode northward, first following the silver rill, then veering away from it as the trail beside it rose higher into the rocky hills toward the distant water source. Veering slightly to the east they found another, broader trail, and even by moonlight Jake could see the recent sign of many horses passing this way. This, then, was the true road into and out of the hidden canyon. They could ride side by side now and so Jake asked in a low voice:

'How many sentries will there be?'

'It varies,' Sarah answered, glancing at him, her dark eyes catching moonlight. 'It depends on how many men Kit thinks he can spare and on how much possible danger he thinks there is.'

That was both good and bad, Jake reflected. He knew Kit Blanchard was now short on men, but he had also been told that the thieves had been pursued southward. So there was a danger that they had been followed toward the canyon.

'I imagine only two or three men,' Sarah guessed.

Well, it could have been worse, he supposed, but two or three men with rifles up among those rocks would be more than formidable. Sarah spoke up again.

'It might be that they won't even see us, Jake. A little farther along there's an old Indian trail that circles that knoll and then drops down toward the flats. It is narrow, but it may be unguarded, because it's unlikely that anyone approaching the canyon would have any idea that it's there.'

Jake could only hope that the girl was right. After another half mile they left the main road, Sarah taking the lead to follow a path which was not much wider than a game trail. It wound sinuously up into the stacked boulders.

She did not hesitate, but walked her pony steadily forward. Jake followed less certainly, his eyes on the rocky surrounding hills, watching for the silhouette of a man and for any movement. Meanwhile, the sky had begun paling in the east, and it seemed certain that they would not be out of the gulch before sunrise tinted the skies. He wanted to urge Sarah on to more speed, but that, too, seemed unwise. A running horse stirs up much dust and the hoofbeats reverberate louder. No, their escape lay in stealth, not in a headlong rush upward.

The trail now crested out and began to wend its way down toward the desert flats. The skies were paling, the stars fading one by one. Jake, glancing eastward, saw the first flash of dawn. A long crimson pennant of thin cloud illuminated the land.

And the rifleman above them opened up.

Even in the poor light the sentries seemed to be able to identify Sarah as a woman, for the shots were not aimed at her. Nevertheless, her roan horse reared up in fright and she was thrown from the saddle to scurry for cover on hands and knees. Jake unsheathed his Henry rifle and kicked free of his stirrups, rushing to Sarah to draw her to the shelter of a dozen man-sized rocks.

The whine of ricocheting bullets was furious, the lead whipping past, singing off stone. Jake wondered if the men above had a real bead on them or were just firing at random. Three rapidly spaced shots ringing off rock not three feet from his head answered that. They knew where they were, all right, and they had them pinned down good and proper.

What would they do now? Logic said that one of the sentries would remain where he was to keep their heads down while the others — how many others? — worked their way down toward where Jake and Sarah were huddled.

Jake glanced around, trying to find an escape route. His buckskin horse, annoyed but loyal, stood its ground nearby, reins trailing. Sarah's frightened roan had raced off down the trail, and now could not be seen.

This meant that even if he had the heart to attempt running, there was no way to escape on horseback.

'What are you going to do?' Sarah asked, her face distraught.

'I don't know. Can you handle a gun?' he asked.

'I don't want to do any shooting,' the woman answered firmly, 'that's why I brought you along.'

'It might be our only way out,' Jake said, as four more bullets peppered the boulders around them, sending rock chips flying.

'Well,' she said calmly, 'if we don't make it, I'll just try again another day.'

'You've tried this before!' he said, stunned by her apparent indifference to their fate.

'Several times.'

And what had happened to her escorts on previous attempts? Maybe she always coaxed the newest man into helping her, the most naive among the crew. He was forced to rethink again what he knew of Sarah and what he believed he knew, or had convinced himself of. Perhaps she was a little mad, or more than a little. He should have listened more closely to Worthy, and to the longtime Blanchard rider, Will Sizemore, when he confided, 'Anything she tells you, you can disbelieve.'

Had he only been duped into playing a role in Sarah's fantasy?

As more bullets flew from upslope, ricocheting off the stones, Jake ducked low and shook his head in wonder. The simple truth now was that it did not matter what Sarah was up to or what she had done before. It was his life as well that he was thinking about, and he had to find a way to get out of the gorge.

'I need you to do some shooting,' Jake said, gripping her shoulder roughly, but Sarah shook her head defiantly

'I don't want to do any shooting. I

told you that! They won't dare hurt me — my cousin, Christi is married to Kit Blanchard.'

'Listen,' Jake Staggs said savagely, leaning near to Sarah. 'It's my life I'm concerned with now! I need you to help me out.'

Her dark eyes had widened and her lower lip trembled as she studied the grim face of Jake Staggs. His hand continued to grip her thin shoulder tightly.

'What do I have to do?' she asked in a strangled voice.

He handed her the Henry repeater and told her, 'Just start firing — not all of the rounds at once, but a few in their general direction. Scoot over a little — you should be able to fire through that notch safely enough.'

'Are you going to . . . ?' she glanced at Jake's patient buckskin horse.

'No, I'm not going to leave you.' Although, he thought, maybe he should do just that. 'I'm going to try to find a better position, with luck somewhere

where they can't see me. Because someone will be coming down after us sooner or later. They can't waste all day just sniping at us.' He again squeezed her shoulder, hard.

'Will you do what I'm asking?' he demanded. She nodded weakly.

'I think so.'

'Then that's what we're going to try. I wish we knew how many men we're up against. Here,' he said, shoving the rifle into her small hands. 'Scoot over to the notch and fire a couple of shots in their general direction, just to keep their heads down. I'm going to slip away toward that little rabbit run over there. See where I mean? When I make it, if I make it, you can quit shooting at them unless you see someone coming this way. But now and then fire off a shot or two just to let them think that we're both still pinned down here.'

'What if it doesn't work?' Sarah asked with apparent concern, though it was getting difficult to read her moods or believe her words. He answered with a

51

touch of cruelty:

'Then you can just go back to the ranch and wait for the next fool crazy enough to try helping you.'

As he watched, Sarah levered a cartridge into the Henry's breech and settled in on her knees. She took aim and fired once, twice. Jake was off in a running crouch before the echoes had died away.

No bullets followed him as he rolled over a low slab of stone and wriggled up between two closely spaced boulders to shelter beside a towering split rock. At the base of the monument was a rabbit run, a trail they used to go from burrow to water or to grass. No wider than a boot, it nevertheless indicated a way up the knoll, for certainly the rabbits knew the hills.

Jake's idea was to work his way higher, and without being seen, to find a place where he could observe any sentry creeping down through the boulders toward Sarah. With luck he would be able to surprise anyone easing his way downslope. Now, still moving in a crouch to keep his own head down, he followed the winding narrow path upward. It was not easy going — where the rabbits could squeeze through narrow splits, Jake had to crawl over the rocks or sometimes detour around the stacked boulders.

The sun rose higher, breaking the plane of the horizon and lifting itself into the dawn sky, erasing the colors of sunrise with its heat and paling the sky as it obliterated the moon's pale glow. A flight of doves winged their way past, presumably toward the rill beyond, and high above a red-tailed hawk circled, searching for its breakfast. Presumably one of the doves. It was all cat and mouse, live or die, out on the desert, and Jake Staggs himself was now one of the players in the eternal game of survival.

Easing up onto a flat boulder, he peered across the rock-strewn slope, searching for movement, his Colt clenched tightly in his hand. He saw nothing and heard only the wind which was rising with the dawn. Squinting into the sunlight he tried to find a trail the sentries might use to work their way down to Sarah's position. At that moment she chose to loose off another rifle shot which whined off of a rock face and sang off into the distance. He knew that she was shooting at nothing, but nevertheless he glanced that way.

And saw the new sun glinting on gun metal not so far from where her bullet had struck. Bare metal winked brightly in the sunlight — one reason most men preferred weapons of blued steel. As the rifleman eased his way downslope, Jake could see him clearly, scuttling from rock to rock, keeping low, his weapon in his hand. That was one of them then, and as Jake continued to watch, the man crept nearer to his own position. Possibly the guard knew of the rabbit run himself. Jake settled in, his palm sweaty as he clenched the pistol grips in his hand with unnecessary pressure.

When the stealthily moving sentry

came nearer, within pistol range now, Jake slowly drew the curved hammer of the Colt back. Were there others around? He had to know, for if he took a shot at the approaching man, he would give his own position away and could expect a barrage of answering fire. But he saw no other men and heard no sounds of movement. His decision was made for him as the stalking man rushed from behind the shelter of one of the yellow boulders, running directly toward Jake's position. He took aim . . .

The second man leaped from a still higher boulder directly onto the rock where Jake lay. Jake Staggs never saw the man's face. Instinctively, however, he rolled onto his back and fired up as the sentry launched himself at Jake, and the guard folded up like an unstrung marionette and tumbled from the rock as the rifleman below fired once, twice, at Jake. Face down against the rock, Jake made a poor target, but the man below, standing erect with his rifle at his shoulder, offered a good target silhouette and Jake fired three times, slamming the gunman back against a rock, the rifle clattering free from his hands. He ended up in a seated position, but he was quite dead, as was the man who had fallen from the rock.

As the gun smoke cleared, Jake frantically thumbed fresh loads into the cylinder of his revolver, searching the slope for a third, or a fourth, or a fifth man, but the day returned to silence. There was no movement, no sound for nearly an hour as the sun rose higher and the desert beyond turned mirror-white. Perspiration trickled into Jake's eyes. He cuffed it away, recovered his hat, and, at length, slipped from the rock. If there had been any other men, they had either made a run for the ranch or withdrawn to some safe bunker. At any rate, there were no more of them near at hand.

Reaching the ground, he paused to look at the man who had fallen there, and as he crouched over him, he heard footsteps and saw Sarah rushing toward him, his rifle in her hand.

'You don't need to see this,' Jake warned her, taking his Henry repeater from her.

'Yes I do!' she said wildly, almost gleefully. 'I need to see both of them.' She crouched down, looked intently at the man's face and nodded with satisfaction. Then, working her way around the boulder she went to where the second man sat, dead eyes staring at eternity. 'Good,' she said with satisfaction.

'Sarah . . . why?' Jake asked weakly. Her face was flushed with excitement when she wheeled to face him.

'Because I know them!' she said wildly. 'I know every man in the gang who has a price on his head — and that's most of them. There's bounty money due us, Jake, and I mean to have it!'

She argued to take the men's bodies along with them, but Jake refused. Sarah had been certain that her roan would return, it knowing only one place on the desert where it could find hay and water — back on the ranch — and she was proved right. By the time they had again reached the buckskin horse, the roan, looking as if it had run itself out, had returned to stand next to Jake's horse.

The girl's spirits were much higher than Jake's as they finally emerged from the rocky hills onto the long desert flats.

'That's two of them,' she said. 'River Tremaine and Lemon Jack. A thousand dollars bounty for the two of them!'

Jake looked at her curiously, and she went on, her eyes fixed on the desert landscape. 'I thought and thought about how I could make my way in this world if ever I left the ranch, and then it came to me — it was so simple. Every one of those men is worth money . . . dead.'

Jake's buckskin was weary again. The land here was high desert, scattered sage and much grease-wood with a few clumps of nopal cactus here and there. Long and dark gray and endless. They followed the tracks of the stolen horses in the opposite direction, northward.

'And when I get the rest of them!' Sarah exulted. 'I'll be a rich woman, won't I, Jake?'

'How are you planning to do that, Sarah?' Jake asked. 'Get the rest of them?'

'I'll get some men to help me. You, of course.'

'Of course not me,' Jake snapped. 'I'm getting the hell out of here and just as fast as I can ride.'

'Are you?' she asked, smiling gently. Ahead now they could make out the low, scattered buildings of Lewiston.

Her question was nonsensical. Of course he was leaving the territory. He had no wish to encounter Kit Blanchard and his gang again. After the buckskin was again rested enough to travel on, he meant to strike out for Nevada or New Mexico Territory. He did not know what he might find there, but he knew one thing: he wanted no part of the madwoman and her schemes, whatever they might be.

4

'Are you sure that coffee is all you want?' the waitress asked with some concern showing on her young, pretty face.

'It's about all I can afford,' Jake Staggs answered.

'Well, it can be a tough world,' she said, not unkindly. Her hair was light brown, almost curly and a little tangled after what must have been a hard day spent on her feet. Jake leaned back, waiting for his coffee, idly studying the other customers, mostly townsmen in their best suits with their ladies in their finery dining and exchanging amusing stories. There was quite a crowd, and it gave Jake pause to wonder whether it might be Sunday or some kind of holiday; he couldn't remember the last time he had seen a calendar.

It can be a tough world, he thought,

and it was not going to get easier any time soon.

* * *

Arriving in Lewiston, Sarah had insisted on going directly to the town marshal's office. The low yellow-brick building with barred windows sat on the edge of town. In an attached jail, also of brick, they could see men with their hands cramped around the bars, staring out hopelessly for assistance.

'Is the marshal here?' Sarah asked, breezing in as if she owned the place. Startled, a young deputy laboring to read the town's one-sheet newspaper, swung his feet from the desk and rose, wiping his hands on his trousers.

'He's here, Miss, but he's not seeing anybody much these days. My name's Bostwick, deputy marshal. Can I help you?'

'Can you authorize payments of a bounty on some men?'

'No,' the thin young deputy said,

wagging his head. 'Only the marshal is authorized to pay rewards and bounties.'

'Then, I wish to see him — you did say that he was here,' Sarah went on eagerly. Jake Staggs watched her, wondering at himself. He had once imagined her to be a sheltered, shy girl. It was a revelation to watch her bull her way in and make her demands. Bostwick, the deputy, nodded and said uncertainly:

'I'll see if Marshal Trouffant will talk to you.' Then he disappeared into the back of the office, leaving Jake and Sarah to stare at the map on the wall, the three or four wanted posters tacked up on a board, the portrait of President Grant which was beginning to sun-fade. It didn't take the deputy all that long. When he emerged, wiping his hands on his trousers yet again — a nervous habit, it seemed — he told Sarah:

'Go on in. It's the second room.'

Sarah marched confidently ahead,

Jake following in her wake. Bostwick gave him a scrutinizing look, his eyes briefly dropping to Jake's holstered Colt, but he said nothing. The corridor they entered was even darker and cooler, despite the heat of the day. Walking directly to the door Bostwick had indicated, she entered. Jake sighed and tagged along.

Inside there was a sort of bedroom with a cupboard, a dressing table, three or four wooden chairs and a rumpled brass bed on which lay a fat, uncomfortable man with a red face.

'Marshal Trouffant?' Sarah asked. She sat in one of the chairs without having been invited. Trouffant looked up and nodded. The man wore a white nightshirt, lay on his side and was in obvious discomfort.

'Good,' Sarah said, ignoring whatever private tortures the marshal might be suffering. 'My name is Sarah Worthy, and I have come to claim the bounty on two members of the Kit Blanchard gang. That is, Lemon Jack and River

Tremaine have both departed this planet.'

'Lemon Jack Baker!' Trouffant said with an eagerness passing through his eyes which then faded to reveal pain again.

'The very same,' Sarah said proudly. 'As I said, he and River Tremaine both. They tried to waylay us out on the desert.'

The marshal frowned. His lower lip pursed as he studied Sarah. 'You did say your name was Worthy?'

'Sarah Worthy, yes.'

'I guess you'd know who they are then. Did you bring the bodies into town for identification?'

'Unfortunately we had only our two horses, but as you said, I can most certainly identify them. They are dead.'

'You were with her?' Trouffant said, shifting his weary eyes to Jake.

'I was,' Jake told the marshal. 'I'm the one that killed them.'

'I see . . . ' the marshal grew thoughtful. He shifted slightly in his bed, but even that small effort seemed to cause him pain. 'You see, I was with the Flagstaff posse when they were pursuing Kit Blanchard. One of the bastards got me in the side with a chance shot. The doctor says it passed clean through, but managed to nick my spine on its way. There's a lot of nerve damage. I'm on laudanum half the time.'

'Sorry,' Jake said, not knowing what other comment he could make.

'I wonder if it was one of those two who shot me,' Trouffant said with bitterness. 'Well, for now let that go. You say you saw the two dead men as well?' the marshal asked Jake Staggs.

'Yes. They are dead. As to their names, I couldn't tell you, but Sarah was sure of their identities.'

'I guess she would be,' Trouffant grumbled.

'So that's settled. When can I expect the bounty on those two to be paid? It was a thousand for the two of them, if I recall. Seven hundred for Lemon Jack . . . '

'It'll be a while,' the marshal said interrupting her. He shifted his position and again winced with pain. 'Would someone hand me that little blue bottle over there? I'm hurtin' pretty bad right now, Miss Worthy; I'll take care of this matter as soon as possible. I'll have to at least talk to the mayor, probably send a letter to the US marshal in Yuma, but I'll see that you get the reward money.'

Sarah wanted to discuss matters further, but Trouffant did not. After only a sip or two from the laudanum he had at hand, his head dropped heavily and no matter that company was present, he flopped back in his bed to fall asleep.

'Let's go,' Jake said in a harsh whisper. 'You got his answer.'

'It doesn't seem right that I should have to wait so long,' she complained. Jake took her arm and turned her out of the room.

'It won't be that long. At least you know you've got your future taken care of for a while.'

'Yes, I have,' she said mysteriously, 'for quite a while to come.'

They walked out past the deputy who was again seated, boots on the marshal's desk, struggling to decode the print on the newspaper page. He watched them with indifference, and perhaps a hint of relief that their visit had caused no problems for him.

It was hot outside, though not searing. Mid-nineties, Jake guessed. The sky was leaden. Only a few people walked the plankwalks of town, only an occasional rider passed. Sarah stopped in the ribbon of shade offered by the porch awning of the marshal's office. She looked up at Jake, stretched out both hands, then let them fall away without touching him.

Her eyes were too intent, overly bright. Mad? She told Jake Staggs:

'Get some rest. By the time Kit Blanchard gets back from Mexico we'll be ready for him.'

Jake rolled a curse around in his dry throat but it would not come to his lips.

Astonishment had strangled it. Tightly, he forced a single word through his teeth:

'What?'

Sarah continued to stare up at him, and her eyes were now those of a woman you wouldn't want to see in the front row of a jury if you were the man on trial. 'You see how easy that was, Jake?' she said lightly. 'A thousand dollars for a few hours work. A thousand isn't much — it isn't near enough. Do you know there's five thousand on Kit Blanchard's head alone? And the rest of the gang — Blanco, Sizemore, Ernie Wright, Ike Sandoval . . . why there's enough money on their heads to set me up for life.'

'And you expect me to go back to Smuggler's Gulch with you?' Jake laughed.

'I don't think *I'd* be much help,' Sarah said. Her expression became vengeful. 'But you could wipe them all out one by one. You don't know how

I've suffered. Why? Because I was never allowed out of the canyon for fear I might give them away! I mean, even as a child, Jake! I've been a prisoner all of my life. Now it's time for them all to pay for it.'

'Turn them into the marshal,' Jake said wearily. He watched an older man and woman drive past in a surrey drawn by a high-stepping sorrel.

'You saw the shape he's in!' Sarah said. 'Besides, lawmen can't collect bounties. You know that.'

Jake shook his head, looked deliberately away and said carefully, 'I am not going to return to Smuggler's Gulch, Sarah. Not for a million dollars in gold, not with fifty armed men at my side. No — you'll have to find another way, one that doesn't include me.'

'I won't!' she exploded. Her dark eyes held fire. 'I have everything planned out and it depends on you. Oh, you'll help me, Jake Staggs,' she said dangerously, 'or I'll make you sorry!'

Her intent was clear in the fierceness

of her words and the slashing light in her eyes, but Jake smiled crookedly, shook his head and challenged her:

'How, Sarah? I helped you out of a situation and I guess I'm glad that I did, but there's no way I'm going back down there and there's nothing you can do to force me to.'

'No?' Her smile was pretty but deadly. 'Where did you say that the buckskin horse you're riding, the one with the Broken T brand on it, came from? You're on the run, aren't you, Jake?' She nearly hissed: 'They still hang horse thieves in this territory. All I have to do is tell the marshal that. Maybe you're no better than Kit Blanchard's men. Maybe you're really one of the gang, and I was afraid to tell him in front of you. They can trace that horse back to its home ranch and see what the owner has to say.'

And, knowing Bert Stiles, Jake knew that the cattleman would be perfectly happy to see him hanged.

With that, Sarah smiled again,

knowingly, turned on her heel and walked away leaving Jake to stare after the small woman in blue jeans. With another girl he might have laughed off her threat, but he was coming to know Sarah far too well. There was no telling what she might resort to to get her way.

★   ★   ★

'I thought you might like a slice of apple pie to go with that coffee,' the waitress said, returning to Jake's restaurant table.

'I can't . . . ' Jake objected.

'You already told me that you're low on funds. I won't see a man go hungry if I can help it.'

Jake nodded his thanks, but she was already gone, moving away to another table where she collected a stack of dishes and returned to the kitchen. Looking around as he shoveled bites of the thick slice of pie into his greedy stomach, Jake saw that the restaurant was filling up rapidly. He couldn't sit there nursing his coffee forever; there were others who wanted the table. He managed to catch the little waitress's eye as she whisked past again, her arm burdened heavily with trays. He held up his lone nickel for her to see, placed it beside his empty plate and rose from his chair. Before he had taken one step he heard her voice behind him.

He turned and watched her slide up behind him. 'Listen, come around to the back of the restaurant in an hour. I'll see that you get a real meal.' She smiled, reached into her apron pocket and said a little more loudly, 'You've forgotten your change, sir.'

A small hand pressed two nickels into his open palm, and before Jake could respond, she had whirled away again, rushing to take an order from two cattlemen in their Sunday best.

Outside the glare of the sun off the glass in the shops along the street was fierce. He did not even glance skyward. The desert sun would be a white ball in the white sky. A yellow dog in the shade of the awning opened its eyes to look at him, wag its tail feebly and go back to sleep. Jake looked at his hand again. The two nickels glinted dully. He had ten cents and an hour to kill. He hoped that the going price in Lewiston was still a nickel for a glass of beer. His parched cells had not yet fully recovered from his long desert trek and the temperature, now over a hundred degrees, was drawing still more moisture from his body. A beer would help. Or two! Hell, he was a rich man for the moment.

It wasn't hard to find a saloon. There were two sitting side by side a block up the street and another opposite. He chose the one on his side of the street to avoid having to leave the band of shade the buildings offered.

Stepping inside the low-ceilinged, musty-smelling building he found a crowd of twenty or so men standing along the bar and another dozen scattered around the tables spaced across the floor. A few were playing cards; others just sat and stared.

One of them was staring directly at Jake Staggs.

It was Blanco.

Jake had never really gotten a good look at the bearded bandit. Most of their time together had been spent with Blanco standing behind him, prodding Jake in the back with the muzzle of his gun, but he recognized Blanco, and if he hadn't, Blanco certainly recognized him. Had he been sent to track Jake down? That could be, since Blanco was the one Kit Blanchard had entrusted to watch Staggs. Either that or Lemon Jack and River Tremaine's bodies had been found. There had been a lot of shooting; someone might have heard it.

Blanco sat alone at the small round table, an empty mug of beer folded between his thick hands. There was absolutely no expression on his dark face which was more unnerving than a flicker of anger or hate would have been. He simply stared, and Jake considered trying to ease his way out of the saloon. No sooner had that thought crossed his mind than a trio of laughing, taunting cowboys came through the batwing doors. In their high spirits they saw nothing wrong. They stood there, blocking the doors. One of them knocked another's hat off and they scuffled good-naturedly for a while as Blanco rose from his table and walked toward Jake Staggs on heavy legs.

'What did you call me!' Blanco roared, and heads turned. The cowboys in the doorway dispersed and stood aside. Jake said nothing. There was no possible answer. Blanco was sketching a thin alibi of self-defense. Jake could only brace himself and wait for the inevitable. Every man in the shabby saloon knew that Blanco was in a killing mood, but since it seemed to be a personal matter, no one tried to stop it.

What Blanco obviously wanted now was to goad or frighten Jake into drawing first. Then, with the combat between two men both unknown to the locals, all they could do was testify that they had heard Blanco object to being called a name and that Jake was the first to go for his gun.

And the temptation to do just that was there. Jake Staggs was not a gun hand. Was Blanco quick to shoot? He did not know that either. All he could do was watch as Blanco stalked him. One voice did speak up saying, 'Take it outside, boys,' but everyone knew it was already too late for that.

Jake licked his dry lips. His eyes briefly unfocused and then locked in on the bulky, bearded man, fixed on his right hand hovering near his holster. Blanco was three strides away when he drew his Colt revolver.

Jake Staggs shot him dead.

Blanco roared in frustration; in pain he threw both hands to his chest where he had been hit and then to his throat where blood was surging up from his ruptured heart, strangling him. Shakily, Jake backed away from the man as he took one staggering step and fell face first to the wooden floor. His leg twitched twice and then the bearded outlaw lay still. The doors behind Staggs swung open again and he looked that way to see the slender Deputy Bostwick, shotgun in his hands, and on his heels Sarah Worthy.

'You got another one!' Sarah cheered, clapping her hands together. 'Deputy, the dead man is Eduardo Blanco, one more of Kit Blanchard's gang, and there's five hundred dollars reward for him!'

Sarah was beaming. Thrilled. She now was dressed in a black velvet dress with red trimming at the hem, cuffs and throat. A tiny matching black and red hat was pinned to her hair. Bostwick, doubtful as ever, lowered his shotgun slightly and told Jake.

'We'd better talk to Marshal Trouffant again.'

Outside, Sarah said, 'You are brilliant, Jake. I knew I'd made the right choice this time.'

'I think his front sight must have

gotten snagged in his holster,' Jake muttered.

'It doesn't matter, does it? Another five hundred dollars!' She hooked her arm around his as they made their way toward the marshal's office, a worried Bostwick trailing.

'How'd you get the new hat and dress?' he asked.

'Oh, I've got money,' she shrugged. 'There was plenty in the house. I knew where they had it stashed.'

Fine. If Kit Blanchard had had no other reason to come after Jake and Sarah, he had one now. She had raided the outlaw gang's treasury.

'You know that I have only two nickels to rub together, Sarah.'

'That will all change soon,' she promised. 'Once the reward money starts rolling in.'

If he lived that long, Jake thought. But she did not offer him any money just then.

If things continued the way Sarah Worthy hoped, she would die a wealthy woman, but a lot of men would die broke along the way.

Marshal Sam Trouffant was still in his bed when they reached the jail, but he looked slightly better.

'I managed to sit up this morning,' he announced proudly. 'Twice, as a matter of fact.' Now his perpetual frown returned, 'The doctor says I'll never ride a horse again, but,' he shrugged, 'Lewiston's all right with me. I like it as well as I'm liable to like any other place. I'll just stay where I am. Now, tell me about the shoot-out.'

Jake related it simply, because in reality there had been nothing dramatic about it. He still believed that Blanco's front sight must have gotten hung up in his holster: the reason many known gunmen filed them off, being of no real use on a handgun anyway.

'Well, at least you did this one the right way,' Trouffant said, shifting again in his bed to try to ease his discomfort. 'I know Blanco's reputation. I've got a circular on him somewhere out in the office — did you find that poster, Bostwick!' he shouted at the deputy, who had not followed them to the marshal's bedroom.

'Where was I?' Trouffant continued after settling into a more comfortable position on his back. 'Yes, you did this one right, Staggs. You see we've got the body right here and he can be identified. Makes the reward claim easier to prove. You might keep that in mind in the future.'

Jake started to interrupt, to assure the marshal that there would be no future bounty claims, not if he could help it. Trouffant didn't give him a chance. He lifted a fat red hand to silence Jake.

'Here is what I am going to ask you to do, son,' he said. 'Bostwick!' The put-upon deputy appeared at the doorway. 'Give it to me,' the marshal ordered.

Staggs assumed that it was the wanted poster that he had asked for, but now the gaunt deputy stepped forward, opened his hand and revealed a shiny deputy marshal's badge like the one pinned to Bostwick's own blue shirt.

'The thing is,' Trouffant said, studying the badge, 'there's already three men dead by your hand, Staggs. People are going to start to wonder if you're not a murderer, some sort of hired killer. So I want you to pin this on before you go after the rest of the gang. That way we're all protected, you see, and we don't have to worry about jailing you for some offense if you have to break the letter of the law to deliver justice to the Kit Blanchard gang.'

Again Jake started to object. Sarah stood by beaming. Deputy Bostwick frowned deeply. Maybe he felt that his authority was to be infringed upon. Trouffant told Jake:

'You don't have to worry about maintaining order here in Lewiston. Bill here knows the people, and he's good enough at his job,' the marshal said, offering Billy a lagniappe. 'No, just wear this badge around here so that people know you're not some outlaw that should be tried for murder. I'll make that appointment retroactive. Then there won't be anything for anyone to get nosy about. You can't know how badly I want to see Kit Blanchard hanged or shot down.' The marshal rubbed his back. 'Look what the bastard did to me! That's your only job, Staggs. Find him and bring him in or shoot him down where he stands, it's all the same to me.

'After you've formulated a plan for going after Blanchard and his gang, come to me and we'll talk it over. You'll doubtless need at least a few good men to ride with you. I can find them.'

For reasons he couldn't fully explain to himself, Jake found himself pinning the deputy's badge on. Perhaps it was the underlying threat — if that was what it was — that Trouffant had made in reminding Jake that he could still be made to stand trial over the death of Blanco, if not of Lemon Jack and River

Tremaine. If the men in the saloon didn't support his story of that shoot out, or if Sarah were to change her testimony concerning the deaths of the other two badmen . . . She was capable of that if she didn't get her way, Jake had no doubt about that now.

'Does this job pay anything?' Jake asked, fingering the shield on his shirt. 'I haven't had a meal since I hit town.'

'Jake!' Sarah said as if speaking to a foolish child. 'Why didn't you say something?' She fished into the tiny reticule she had on her wrist. 'Here, make sure to get yourself a good meal. We can't risk having you weaken on us.'

Jake took the small ten-dollar gold coin she slipped from her purse and pocketed it. Sarah continued to gaze at the badge on his shirt front with appreciation which he didn't under-stand for a while, until it occurred to him that she no longer had to consider him a partner, since, as had been pointed out, a lawman cannot claim a bounty or reward. And that was what he now was, like it or not: a lawman.

Just like the disabled Sam Trouffant who also could not legally claim any part of the reward money. However, the marshal seemed inordinately proud of himself as well, which made no sense, unless the marshal was now Sarah Worthy's new partner. If he was, well, God help him. He may have thought he had met the devil when he ran across Kit Blanchard, but Sarah Worthy could teach the world what a hellion was.

5

Jake hadn't expected to find her there. By the time he managed to return to the rear of the restaurant one hour had stretched to two, but there she stood, patiently waiting for him in the heated shadows of the late desert afternoon.

'Hello,' the waitress said. Noticing the badge on his shirt front she commented, 'It seems you've had a busy day already.'

'Things change quickly, Miss . . . '

'Cathy will do. Cathy Vance.'

They faced each other hesitantly. Jake appreciated the way her plain blue calico dress fitted her slender body, the shy way her eyes drifted toward his and then away again. What she was thinking as she studied the rangy, desert-hardened man before her he could not guess.

'You offered me a kindness,' Jake said.

'I hadn't a nickel and you offered to help.'

'We're put on earth to help one another,' Cathy said simply, and there was sincerity in her words.

'What I am getting at,' Jake said, removing his hat briefly to scratch at his head, 'is that I'm now in a position to buy you a meal if you are hungry.'

'I'm not really starved, are you?'

'If there's a stronger word for it, I am,' Jake laughed. 'That piece of pie is all I've had to eat in a long time.'

'Well, then, let's feed you,' Cathy said. As Jake started toward the restaurant door, she touched his arm. 'Not in there. I spend every day and sometimes half the night in there. If you'll trust my cooking, I can make you something at home.'

Jake nodded agreement. That seemed to be what the lady wanted, and he found the suggestion agreeable. So long as he satisfied his stomach, it made no difference just now. He walked with Cathy to the next street where they turned left, away from the town. The sun was hot, there were the bright chirps of cicadas along the dry riverbed. There was a row of dusty salt cedar trees planted as a windbreak along the road, and their shade offered some respite from the glare of the high sun. Cathy told him:

'It's not that long a walk. We have a small cabin up ahead. I share it with my two room mates — two other waitresses.'

Not much later they came upon a small white clapboard house, the paint on the sun side of the house sun-blistered and peeling. The picket fence was missing a few slats. Beside the three narrow steps leading up to the green front door someone had planted roses inside rings of white-painted rock. The roses looked wilted and desperate, struggling to survive in the desert heat. A red dog with a broom tail started around the corner at their approach, then turned and slunk away. Cathy laughed.

'That's Chaser. He came with the house. He doesn't seem to like anybody very much.'

'Maybe there's a reason,' Jake said, and Cathy glanced at him oddly as she fished a key out of her small blue purse and opened the front door.

'Better leave the door open,' she said. 'It's hotter in here than it was outside. Usually a breeze comes up at this time of day. It will do something to cool us down.'

She was right. The interior of the house was nearly stifling, but after Cathy had crossed to the other side of the cabin and opened the back door as well, a slight breeze shifted the heat out, enough to make it bearable.

'I hate coming home when the place has been closed up all day,' Cathy said as she removed her hat, took the pins from her hair and shook her head so that it tumbled down across her shoulders. 'That's better already,' she said with a smile. 'What I usually do is make a plate for myself and sit outside in the shade of the cottonwoods — if that's not too informal for you.'

'Cathy, there's almost nothing that's too informal for me,' Jake said, thinking of the meals — if they could be called that — that he had eaten on the desert, tasteless and filled with blow sand, eaten only to keep himself alive.

'All right,' she said, 'I won't be long. I'm not going to make anything elaborate.' She retrieved an apron from a hook and tied it on. Jake sat at a kitchen chair, enjoying the sight of a woman about her everyday work. It was something he had not experienced much in his wandering life. Beyond the back door he could see three mature cottonwood trees, now swaying in the breeze. Their seedpods blew like miniature clouds. He spotted Chaser once, lounging in the shade. The dog looked up, appeared to notice Jake Staggs watching him and skulked away. Beyond the yard lay the dry creek clogged with willow brush, then the gray desert began, stretching out forever before meeting the low, craggy foothills in the far distance.

'I've got all you're going to get,' Cathy said with a somewhat rueful smile. In her hands was a large platter holding sliced ham, a wedge of cheese, bread and a jar of jam. 'If you could have waited until it cooled down . . . I hate to stand cooking over that stove on a summer day.'

'That looks fine,' Jake assured her. It couldn't have looked finer, he thought, as she led the way outside to a small, roughly built table with a bench on either side. It was still diabolically warm, but the shade from the cotton-woods and the rising breeze made it a pleasant spot to picnic, especially for a man who was bordering on ravenous hunger.

She said little as he ate, perhaps not wanting to interrupt him. She smiled faintly as if pleased with herself for having taken care of him. The shadows grew longer, the evening coolness began to settle.

When Jake was nearly finished with his meal Cathy returned to the house, emerging with a glass of milk and a wedge of apple pie. He took a bite of the pie and looked up at her questioningly.

'Taste familiar?' she asked with a laugh. 'It should. It's the same as the restaurant serves. I make them to earn a little extra money.'

When he was finished, Jake pushed plate and glass away and stretched his arms, thanking the woman with deeply felt gratitude. She waved his thanks away and busied herself cleaning off the table. While she was in the kitchen, Jake amused himself by trying to lure Chaser out of concealment. The dog's eyes seemed eager and then wary. It would lift itself on its haunches and then slink away again, hiding in the shadows. Cathy caught them at their game.

'I think someone must have beat him at one time,' she said. 'I don't know. All we do is put food out for him in the morning. He never comes near any of us.'

'You're probably right,' Jake said, tilting his hat back as he straightened in his chair. 'It's a shame what some people will do to animals. And to each other.' He looked at Cathy who sat on the bench opposite, her hands folded together, eyes turned downward. Her lips trembled as if she were attempting to speak, but she made no sound. 'What is it, Cathy? Is something troubling you?'

'It's just . . . ' Jake prompted her with his eyes. 'They say that you are a killer, Jake.'

'They say . . . who? Are you talking about that trouble in the saloon today?'

'And other things,' she said hesitantly. 'Those two men you killed for the bounty on their heads.'

'How could anyone know about that!'

'It's a small town, Jake,' Cathy said. 'Does any of this have anything to do with why you're wearing a badge now?'

'Yes,' he said sighing heavily, 'it does. If you really want to know what happened, I'll tell you, though it will be long in the telling.'

'I want to know, Jake,' she said, glancing toward the corner of the yard where Chaser was again stirring uncertainly. And so Jake settled in and told her about it all from back to front, leaving nothing out. By the time he was finished the western sky was purpling with dusk and it was almost cool beneath the trees where they sat.

'Then she really is mad,' Cathy said at last.

'So it seems.'

'Do they know what caused it?'

'Worthy told me that he thought that it was the desert that did it.'

'I can almost believe that,' Cathy said, her voice subdued, her eyes now fixed on a faraway point on the horizon. 'It gets to me sometimes,' she admitted, 'living here.' She brightened as if sharing a long-held dream, 'No one has to stay here, you know. Not far to the north is Flagstaff. It's higher up — pine trees grow thickly there. You could go there . . . ' She stumbled over the last word which was formed on her lips as 'too.' Jake Staggs shook his head.

'No, I can't. Not the way things are now.' He told her, 'If Sarah changes her mind about her testimony I could be tried for murder. Guilty or not, it's not an ordeal I wish to go through. If Marshal Trouffant were to decide that I was crossing him, he could bring charges against me for shooting Blanco. Then there's the matter of that Broken T horse I'm riding. Horse stealing is not kindly looked upon. They've got me in a trap, Cathy. If I made a run for Flagstaff or anywhere else, they'd have fliers out on me with a description of me and the buckskin before I could get out of Arizona.

'Cathy,' he told the small girl who watched him steadily with her soft brown eyes, 'I more or less have the choice between going along with whatever they have in mind or getting myself hanged.'

After that they found little to talk about. Jake did ask for a few bits of ham fat, and as darkness began to settle he continued to urge Chaser to emerge from his hiding spot. At length the red dog came forward, crawling on its belly to sniff Jake's proffered hand. Then with a sudden lunge and snap of strong jaws, the dog took the ham, narrowly missing Jake's fingers, and raced back to the shelter of the bushes. The dog eventually started forward again, but there was a sudden bustle and commotion in the house. Jake glanced that way to see two other young women, Cathy's house mates, entering the house, unpinning their hats, and laughing and complaining at once. Chaser darted away at the burst of activity, and Jake rose to his feet himself. It was time to make his way back to town and see what devilry Sarah had devised.

He went to the back porch and waited, not in the mood to be

introduced to two chattery females, and eventually Cathy came out, looking faintly apologetic.

'I'm sorry, Jake,' she said, standing near to him in the shadowed yard.

'What for? It's their home. Besides, all you promised me was a meal, and that was much appreciated. That and having someone to talk to for just a little while.'

'It does make a difference, doesn't it?' Cathy said, looking away. 'Just having someone to talk to?'

Then, before Jake could react she went on tip-toes, kissed his cheek and turned to scurry back into the house, softly closing the door behind her.

'I'll be damned,' he said, lightly touching his cheek with his fingertips. Grinning, he made his way around the house back to the road as sundown colors flourished against the long skies. He was a hundred feet or so along the road when he had the feeling that he was being followed. He turned hopefully — maybe Cathy had decided to catch up with him, but there was no one there. Nothing to be seen. Except some movement in the shadows which took substance in the form of Chaser.

The red dog looked at him, turned and hid, then returned. 'Well, make up your mind! Come along if you want to!' Jake said, slapping his thigh, but Chaser turned and dashed toward home. Jake smiled, shook his head and walked on toward Lewiston and its devils.

* * *

The hotel room was small, square and badly painted. But it came with the use of a bath downstairs in the back of the hotel, and Jake didn't begrudge the money whittled from his total fortune of ten dollars courtesy of Sarah Worthy. And where, he wondered, as he soaked the trail dirt from his body and eased the pain of a dozen heavy bruises with the hot water, had Sarah gotten to? There was no telling. Maybe, he thought, she had just given into her madness and was now out in the desert tearing her hair from her scalp, rending her garments, spinning in circles as she raved at the moon.

He knew it was not so, but it was a comforting, if fantastic vision.

No, he thought as he rose from the tub and took the towel from the pudgy man who worked there, Sarah would be around. Whatever her madness had once been it had transmuted into an obsession over money. Jake toweled himself roughly, losing a few layers of skin, dressed again and walked slowly toward the staircase leading to his room, still thinking about Sarah.

How could he not?

The woman was determined that Jake was the man to return to Smuggler's Gulch, capture or ambush Kit Blanchard's gang and claim the bounty on their heads for her. The only problem was, there was no way in the world that Jake intended to attempt any such thing. No matter how many deputies Trouffant thought he could gather — and from the size of the town he doubted that many men could be found who were willing to volunteer to shed their blood in that godforsaken canyon — it was a hazardous proposition.

When he returned from Mexico, Kit Blanchard would be furious. There had been two guards posted on the high bluffs at the entrance to the gulch when Jake had made his way out. Kit would double or triple the number of sentries hiding among those boulders now. All practiced marksmen, outlaws used to killing, and at the first sign of trouble, other men would rush to join them.

It would take an army, and a competent one, to fight its way into Smuggler's Gulch.

Jake lay on his bed, hands behind his head staring at the ceiling of his room as the Arizona skies went from deep purple to star-pierced black. He wondered at the differences between Sarah Worthy and Cathy Vance. All Cathy wanted was to live decently, preferably somewhere where the harsh desert winds did not blow away her expectations. All Sarah Worthy wanted was . . . everything.

Given the chance, and possessing the means, Jake would have packed Cathy up and taken her to Flagstaff or somewhere else — it did not matter where, and helped her find her place in the world. He expected nothing from the girl; he really knew her not at all, but it would make him feel proud that for once in his miserable life he had helped someone. But he could not do that. As he had explained to Cathy, Marshal Trouffant and Sarah would have posters out on him the minute he breached what they saw as a contract to bring Kit Blanchard down.

Jake closed his eyes, dozed for a few minutes during which he suffered through a dream of himself rushing out madly into the desert and tearing out his hair in frustration.

A few minutes rest was all he needed. It was too early for true sleep, and there was too much clogging his mind. Try again to have a beer at the saloon? He rose, yawned, stood in front of the bluish, tilted mirror, studying his distorted image. He rubbed his jaw. He still had not shaved.

All right then — a barber shop, maybe visit an emporium to buy a new shirt. Then a beer or even two and try to get a decent night's sleep, perhaps waking in the morning with an idea of how to get himself out of this mess which didn't involve simply spurring the buckskin away as quickly as possible. Thinking of the buckskin took him first to the shabby stable where he and Sarah had left their horses. The buckskin was there, and in an adjacent stall stood Sarah's roan. The buckskin eyed him hopefully but with that mingled bit of distrust its eyes usually held. What now? the look seemed to convey, and it was true that Jake had not used the animal easily.

Seeing that hay remained in its rick and that there was a bucket of fresh water, Jake stroked the sturdy horse's neck, pondering. He had not entirely abandoned the idea of simply fleeing. But by the time he could reach Yuma they likely would already have a description of him and the stolen horse. Nor could he flee to Mexico, being a well-known *yanqui* burro-killer. It seemed there was nothing that could be done except to try to follow through with the mad plan to capture Kit Blanchard. Maybe Sarah would come to realize that her idea could not work, but Jake doubted she could be made to recognize any reality.

Uptown he let himself be shaved and dusted with talcum powder from the barber's brush. He found an open store and bought a light blue- and white-checked shirt, disposing of his torn old one in the store's trash. Then, bathed and barbered, his marshal's badge pinned to his crisp new shirt he went out into the desert night, wondering what new torments it might be concealing.

He thought of returning to the restaurant, but he knew full well that Cathy's shift had ended. He even thought of walking out to her house once more. But arriving unannounced, with two other girls there probably in various states of undress, seemed a poor idea.

He returned to his first thought, and walked along the boardwalk toward one of the side-by-side saloons across the street from where the earlier dispute had occurred. He was superstitiously uneasy about returning to the establishment where he had killed Blanco.

The saloon, the Golden Eagle a sign proclaimed, seemed to hush for a moment as Jake entered, but that might have been imagination, for it was a roaring boisterous place as he made his way toward the bar, poker chips clicking, men slapping down cards with a curse or a yell of delight, the constant sound of glass against glass and the occasional breaking of the same. There was no piano and no such thing as a bar girl to be seen. The town was too far west and too new to offer these refinements.

There was a line of greasy looking men, mostly bearded, ranked along the bar when Jake edged his way to it. They eyed him, looked away again and returned to their drinking, except for one bearish man with gray whiskers and a balding head who continued to glower. Jake ignored him and ordered a beer from the narrow, harried barkeep.

The mug arrived, Jake wrapped his hand around the glass and the bald man said roughly, 'Are you supposed to be the law here?'

Jake glanced at the badge on his shirt, at the big man and at his amused friends and nodded. 'I suppose so.' He turned his back to them deliberately and asked the bartender, 'Isn't there any place in this town where a man can have a beer in peace?'

The barkeep didn't smile. He only eased away as the big, balding man moved nearer to Jake.

'I'm Hutch Gleason,' he said.

'I congratulate you,' Jake said expressionlessly, stretching out his hand again toward the mug of amber liquid he had been served.

'I heard you rode with Kit Blanchard,' the man called Hutch Gleason said, raising his voice.

'You heard wrong,' Jake said quietly.

'I heard Kit Blanchard is a dirty horse thief,' Gleason persisted.

'He seems to be,' Jake agreed.

'In fact he took some of my animals, blood stock.'

'We'll bring him in for it,' Jake replied. 'Your ponies are likely in Mexico by now, though.'

'How would you know that?' Gleason asked obnoxiously.

'I'm talking about the odds of it.'

'What about the odds of you catching him?' Gleason, obviously drunk, moved still nearer. At the tables and along the bar men watched. It was cheap entertainment, after all.

'We'll try.' Jake again reached for his

beer mug, but Gleason stretched an arm around him and swatted it away. The mug slid along the polished surface of the bar, caught the rim and tipped over, falling to the floor.

'I hear you gunned down Eduardo Blanco. I'm a lot better with a gun than Blanco ever was.'

Jake only nodded and said carefully, 'I'm sure you are.'

'You wouldn't want to try me,' Gleason continued.

'No, I wouldn't.'

'If I wanted to, I could break you in half with my bare hands.'

Staggs nodded. 'I wouldn't doubt that either, you're probably twice as strong as I am.'

'Are you mocking me!' Gleason bellowed. He lunged forward, infuriated or motivated by a need to impress his friends. Either way, he was a big, dangerous, out of control man. Jake took half a step back, braced himself against the bar and kicked Gleason in the kneecap as hard as he could. When

Gleason groaned and bent forward to hold his knee Jake smashed down on his nose with his forearm. The crack of the blow could be heard across the now silent barroom, and Jake wondered for a moment if he hadn't broken his own arm. But it was Gleason's nose that had suffered and it spewed crimson blood as the big man looked up at Jake briefly, his eyes wide with astonishment, before he pitched forward on his face to land against the floor not far from where Jake's empty beer mug lay.

Jake repeated his question to the barkeep: 'Isn't there any place in this town where a man can have a beer in peace?'

The bartender backed away mutely, fear in his eyes and Jake shrugged and stepped over the fallen Gleason. He made his way to the door and stepped out into the cool of the desert night as the uproar within gathered new momentum and volume. The doors swung shut behind him and he started on his way, more certain now than ever that he did not wish to be a lawman in Lewiston and equally certain that he could not remain long on the desert if he were to have any hope of surviving.

6

Jake awoke in his hotel bed as the first silver light of dawn pierced the devil sky roofing the desert. He rose feeling weary, dejected and defeated as he had every right to feel. He dressed with a sullen anger coiled inside him. Where had everything gone wrong? He would have liked to go to the restaurant, flirt with Cathy Vance, laugh and later look around for honest work.

But he was a deputy marshal assigned to track down a bloody killer or risk having his own neck stretched.

What else could a notorious burro-killer expect out of life?

Still, there was nothing for it but to vacillate and wriggle, to try to convince both Sarah and the marshal that an assault on Smuggler's Gulch was a recipe for disaster, because that was exactly what it was. Marshal Trouffant could possibly be persuaded of that, but Sarah . . . she was Sarah. Jake wasn't sure if it was vengeance or gold-lust that drove her, but either way she had no apparent objection to men dying as long as she achieved her ends.

Jake's stomach complained that it was hungry as he stepped out into the low silver light of the morning, but there was a bad taste in his mouth overriding the impulse to eat. He stalked the plankwalk toward Trouffant's office, still wondering if the bed-ridden marshal had not decided that a liaison with Sarah Worthy was a path to his own financial security. Obviously he could not hold office for much longer, the shape he was in, and he must have deep concerns about his own seemingly doomed livelihood. He had certainly seemed over-eager to pin a badge on a man he knew nothing about except that he had been responsible for the deaths of three wanted men.

'Me,' Jake muttered to himself. 'A

real gun dog, dark angel of retribution. Gunfighter and bounty killer.' Except he was none of those. All he wanted was out of Lewiston, out of Arizona and as far away as he could possibly get from Kit Blanchard and the Smugglers Gulch gang.

There were a dozen horses drawn up in front of the marshal's office and the sick feeling in Jake's belly deepened. He knew already . . .

'Good morning,' Deputy Bostwick said in greeting. The young man was smirking with amusement. 'The marshal is waiting for you — with news about your posse.'

Jake trudged down the short corridor toward the marshal's bedroom. Several rough-appearing men in dirty range clothes lounged along the walls. Jake ignored their scornfully appraising glances and proceeded into Trouffant's room, finding four or five other men gathered around the marshal's bed. At least, he thought thankfully, Sarah Worthy was not there.

But Hutch Gleason was.

The big balding man wore a strip of adhesive tape across his nose. One nostril was packed with cotton, and both of his eyes were blackened.

'Good morning, Staggs,' the marshal said from his bed. He was propped up on a pair of pillows and seemed better than the last time Jake had visited him. 'I was hoping you'd drop around. This is Hutch Gleason — oh, you two have already met. I'd forgotten. He owns the Cat's Cradle Ranch north of here, and he's volunteered to bring in some of his hands to assist you in your pursuit of Kit Blanchard and his gang.'

Jake glanced around at the trail-dusty men. Gleason's expression was more than hostile. He said nothing but breathed heavily through his mouth as he stared at him.

'It's not possible,' Jake said to the marshal. 'The entrance to the canyon is heavily guarded. The number of men in our force means nothing. There'll be sharpshooters posted in the rocks above. Any posse trying to enter will be picked off one by one like clay pigeons.'

'That's your opinion?' Trouffant said wearily. He shifted to ease the pain in his back.

'That's the fact of the matter. The place is a fortress.'

'Miss Worthy tells it differently,' Trouffant rumbled. 'She tells me that you know another way into the gorge, one which isn't guarded.'

'I stumbled upon it,' Jake answered. 'It was sheer chance. To reach it, you'd have to ride thirty miles south and climb the face of the hills from the low desert.'

'You did it,' Hutch Gleason said sullenly.

'One man might do it — one man unexpected and apparently harmless. But a posse, their intent clear . . . it can't be done.'

'Are you a coward?' Trouffant asked softly. Jake shook his head. No, at least he thought not, but to risk his life for someone else's profit was insane.

'Courage has nothing to do with it,' he answered.

'I think it does,' Hutch Gleason said. Now with his rough-looking cronies siding him, the big man's blustering manner had returned. Jake found himself wishing that he had beaten all of the fight out of Hutch the night before. Gleason continued, 'Kit Blanchard stole some of my finest blood stock — it's said that he doesn't stoop to rustling mustangs. I figure I'm out four or five thousand dollars at the least. Now some Mexican vaqueros are astride my Kentucky-bred horses. I won't stand for it. I want the man dead!'

'It can't be done,' Jake repeated definitely.

'Oh, it can be,' Marshal Trouffant said jabbing a stubby finger at Jake Staggs, 'or there will be at least one horse thief hanged in this town!'

Jake knew what he meant. The nemesis of the Broken T horse he rode still hung over him. He could not explain all about Bert Stiles and how he had cheated him out of his wages. Well, he could have, but these men did not care a whit. Perhaps a judge and jury might listen and understand, but that was too big a risk to take.

'All right,' Jake Staggs said quietly. 'Since it seems I have no choice, we'll try it. Just tell this man,' he said nodding toward Hutch Gleason, 'that I am the one wearing the badge and I am the one in charge.'

★   ★   ★

'You're leaving town?' Cathy asked in a low voice as she placed a platter of fried potatoes, eggs and sausage in front of Jake. The restaurant was more deserted on this morning than it had been the day before. Only a few men who might or might not have been a part of the posse sat at the scattered tables, drinking coffee or finishing their breakfasts. 'When will you be back?' she inquired with a hint of

115

concern in her voice and in her light brown eyes.

'I doubt that I'll be coming back,' Jake answered.

'Why?' she asked. Looking around uneasily, she apparently broke a rule when she shifted her skirt and sat down facing Jake, her small hands folded together on the table. 'Don't you want . . . ?'

'It's not a matter of what I want,' Jake said. 'I told you most of it yesterday, but it's gotten worse. They're convinced that I have secret knowledge that can guide a posse into Smuggler's Gulch and capture or kill Kit Blanchard.'

'But you don't?'

'No, I do not.'

'Then where did the idea come from?' Cathy said. 'Oh, I see — from the girl, Sarah Worthy.'

'Yes.'

'Is it Kit Blanchard she wants dead — or you?'

'I don't think it really matters to her,' Jake replied.

'I think she's sick . . . and evil!' Cathy exploded.

Jake answered quietly, 'I think you're right.'

His breakfast, as nourishing and necessary as it was, had no taste. Jake waited until he was sure that Cathy Vance was in the restaurant kitchen, plunked down two silver dollars, and left before they could speak again. He had no idea what to tell her and he could not stand seeing the anguish in her eyes.

They were all there waiting for him at the stable. Some men stood outside, a few had already mounted, some were inside the dark structure, saddling their ponies, tightening cinches or adjusting their stirrups. Hutch Gleason stood near the doorway, his face shadowed, his back turned to the brilliant sunlight of the desert morning. The big man said nothing, but after Jake had saddled the buckskin and swung aboard, Gleason shouted to his men.

'It's time, boys, let's get going!' And

despite what Jake had been promised, it was obvious that Gleason saw himself as commander of their small force. They trailed slowly out of town toward the east, the way to the low desert, and suddenly she was there, shouting and waving:

Sarah Worthy in a white dress with red ribbon trimming followed them along the boardwalk for a way, waving a handkerchief and yelling out:

'Give 'em hell, boys!'

Jake was reminded of his boyhood when he had watched a volunteer Confederate regiment from his home town ride down the street, dozens of young, brave men, crisp in their new gray uniforms, all doomed to die, passing while the band played 'Dixie' and ladies with their bright parasols on their shoulders blew kisses.

It was no different; this, too, was a lost cause before it had even begun.

The white sand desert stretched out endlessly to the east, and ahead were only the stony sentinels surrounding the canyon known as Smuggler's Gulch where twenty armed men waited. Or did not — no one could predict what Kit Blanchard might have done. He was hardly a stupid man, and he might have suspected or had spies who had informed him that a posse had been formed to try assaulting the outlaw stronghold.

It could be that even then as the posse labored its way through blown sand, the white sun glaring down, that Kit Blanchard and his mob were sitting safely somewhere in Mexico in the shade of jacaranda trees, sipping cool drinks while dark-eyed smiling *señoritas* waited on them.

The wind continued to increase, and glancing to the north Jake saw a dark ominous ridge of brown clouds. They were likely to find themselves in the middle of a hard sandstorm if they could not get to shelter. And there was no shelter. He urged the plodding buckskin on, bowing his head and closing his eyelids to slits. Now all of the riders had pulled their bandanas up over mouth and nose. Each of them could feel the rising hot wind, see the swirl of sand around them and they knew what was coming. In the midst of a hard desert sandstorm, seeing and breathing could become impossible. Horses suffocated, men died.

Hutch Gleason, his face masked with his red kerchief was beside Jake and shouted, 'Where the hell is this trail? You're supposed to know the way!'

'I can't see it. All of this,' Jake waved a hand around at the rocky slopes, 'looks the same, doesn't it?'

'I'm glad we followed you,' Gleason said sarcastically.

'No one asked you to!' Jake yelled back.

The wind rose with still greater ferocity. Heavy sand moved past them at a height of fifty feet or more. The white sun went yellow, red and then faded behind the brown sand veil. Jake had the feeling that he was riding alone — he could not even make out the silhouettes of the men beside and behind him. How was he supposed to find the lost trail? His earlier thought, as thin a hope as it was, was that the hoofprints his buckskin horse had left on his first visit to the gorge could be followed; now there was no hope of that as the sand covered all signs of earlier passing.

The wind seemed to lessen. Jake opened his sand-stung eyes enough to find the reason. He was now riding near the base of the boulder-strewn hillrise so that it cut the wind. Something about the terrain seemed familiar, but he could not make a certain determination. The buckskin seemed to want to move more quickly. Its ears were pricked, its hoofs danced across the sand.

'Is this it?' Jake asked the animal. 'Do you remember the way?'

The way to shelter and water and fodder. Perhaps the horse remembered. Jake let the buckskin have its head as he squinted back through the smothering darkness of the sandstorm. Wherever the others were, they were no longer beside him. The buckskin picked its way upward through the rocks, having an instinct for the once-used trail, and for better or worse, Jake Staggs was once again bound for Smuggler's Gulch alone.

The sandstorm was not going to blow itself out quickly, but as the horse took him higher onto the hill, Jake could see across the brown layer of dust to the far mountains. If there were men below, perhaps following him, he could not tell. Nothing could be discerned but the rising rocky ridge above, and below, the endless blanket of moving sand.

The buckskin moved on obstinately, and now Jake believed he recognized the few landmarks that there were himself. A split boulder here, a somehow-familiar mound of red rocks. If this was a good sign or not, he didn't know — what pleasure could he find in arriving alone once again at the outlaw camp? What would they ask; what could he say? He would be lucky if Kit Blanchard didn't just gun him down out of hand.

The hot wind did not cease, but the sand did not blow up over the crest of the hills into Smuggler's Gulch — for that was certainly where he was now. The trickle of the rill, the long stand of ragged Mexican fan palms, the sycamores in the bottom of the canyon, and nestled in a feeder canyon, the stone house. Now what was he to do?

Jake found himself in a place he didn't wish to be with no place to escape to but somewhere else he did not wish to be.

A man can build strange prisons for himself.

He started toward the house. The buckskin, unaware of its rider's misery, seemed eager to reach the ranch. There, it knew, was water and hay and a place to shelter from the hot wind. Jake viewed it as a descent into hell, which it likely was. He slowed the buckskin to a walk and made his way through the cottonwood grove, now bleak and arid as the devil winds punished it.

She rushed from the shelter of the trees, threw both hands high and pleaded:

'Save me, oh, save me!'

Jake halted the uneasy buckskin and gawked as the disheveled blonde Christiana Blanchard came running toward him.

She was breathing hard as she reached the horse, took hold of the bridle and panted, 'They're liable to kill me; you must get me away from here.' Then she looked more closely, recognized Jake Staggs and said as if it made no difference to her, 'Oh, it's you.'

'It's me,' Jake was forced to admit. 'What's going on here?' He swung down from the horse not out of politeness, but simply to relieve his cramped leg muscles. She followed him to the same side of the horse and took his hands, much as Sarah had once done, looking up at him in the same panicked way, except that her eyes were deep blue whereas Sarah's were black as coal.

'It's Kit,' she said excitedly. 'He came back in a fury. I think he's going to kill someone — possibly me!'

'What's he so mad about — surely not Sarah's having run off . . . '

'With all his money! Do you know how much she took?' Christiana asked.

'I have no idea. I didn't know anything about what she'd done until we reached Lewiston.'

'That may be, but I don't think you'd want to try to convince Kit of that — with the money missing and two of his men dead.'

'Three,' Jake told her. 'Blanco won't be coming back either.'

'Three, then. I don't know if I can convince Kit that none of this was my doing, Sarah being my cousin. You — if you get caught here, he'll kill you for sure.'

Jake lifted his eyes toward the house in the valley. 'Where is Kit now?'

'Gone again, but for how long I can't say. He doesn't tell me his plans anymore. It's not like it used to be. He now thinks that I'm untrustworthy too. That's the way outlaws always get, isn't it? Trusting no one.'

'I wouldn't know, but yes, it seems so.' Jake paused, glanced up the backtrail to see if Hutch Gleason and the posse had somehow tracked him up here, then looked again at Christiana Blanchard who had only now let go of his hands.

'What is really the matter with Sarah?' he asked.

'God knows. She's gotten worse over the years. She even stole my yellow shirt to wear before she left here. Is that rational! Why would she do that? There are all sorts of small objects missing from my room.' She ran her fingers through her blonde hair; her eyes were still wild.

'What about Worthy? Is he all right?' Jake asked with some concern.

'My uncle's well enough, though his

strength seems to be fading — it's partly age, I suppose, partly because Sarah deserted him.'

'Will he be safe here with Kit on a rampage?'

Christiana shook her head vigorously. And, apparently anticipating what Jake would have asked next, she told him, 'He'll never leave the gulch. It's his home, his land. A man gets attached to such things. When Kit and I first got here he was so pleased to see us — he looked on Kit as the son he had never had. He didn't know what Kit had in mind.'

'Making an outlaw camp out of the gorge.'

'Exactly. Now things are taking a bad turn. I just want out of here, Jake! You can take me — you've made it through before. Of course,' she added with the venom only an angry female can put into her words, 'If I encounter Sarah, I shall kill her on sight.'

7

Jake took Christiana's words and studied the hatred in her eyes, but he said nothing at that moment to try to calm her down. He had more important matters to consider, like staying alive himself. Somewhere behind him was Hutch Gleason and his posse; somewhere below Kit Blanchard and his outlaw band. Somewhere in the far distance Marshal Trouffant would be waiting, ready to hang him if he failed, and Sarah, perhaps waiting to be killed by her pretty cousin.

And somewhere Cathy also watched and waited, or so he hoped.

'Worthy told me that you know a secret way out of the canyon,' Christiana Blanchard was saying.

'If you mean back toward the east, we can't use the trail. There's an army of men looking for Kit down there.'

'Then the road you traveled when you took Sarah out of here.'

'I don't think I could fool them twice going that way — as everyone says, Kit is not a stupid man. He'll have the guards alerted to the Indian cut-off.'

'There might be another way!' Christiana said, her eyes gathering excitement. 'I think I might just know one. Sarah has ridden these hills from childhood. Well, she and I used to ride a lot together, just wandering around, talking of woman things. There's a ridge beyond the falls that feeds the rill. I've never gone all the way up and over, but it could be done. I'm sure of it.'

'Are you sure you want to escape, Christiana?' Jake asked. 'Kit is liable to track you down. He might take your flight as evidence that you and Sarah were plotting together to steal the gang's treasury.'

Plus, Jake was thinking, how could he trust this woman? Kit Blanchard's woman. Did he really want to ride the long land with her? No. But he had to escape from Smuggler's Gulch. There were no two ways about that.

'He might catch up with me and kill me,' Christiana said with a sorrowful shrug, 'or he might decide just to kill me here. He knows where to find a woman to quickly replace me — in Mexico — and he has the money to satisfy one.'

Jake said nothing. He could sense that Christiana now felt like nothing more than chattel; to be used or discarded at will by Kit Blanchard. He could sense her fear and deep mistrust. He considered deeply, realizing he knew little about women — look at the mistake he had made in trusting Sarah Worthy! But a man can't let past mistakes cloud his better impulses. He told her:

'If you've got a horse, I'm ready to ride.'

What choice did he have?

If the wind blew fiercely on the desert, no breeze even touched them in the long valley. It was hot, airless.

Christiana Blanchard led the way, seeming eager to get as far away as possible, as quickly as possible. As was Jake for that matter, but he did not have the faith she apparently had that escaping from Smuggler's Gulch would settle all of his problems.

There was still the law. There was still the belligerent Hutch Gleason who had probably decided by now that Jake had intentionally slipped away from them during the sandstorm, probably to warn Kit Blanchard of their approach.

Christiana was wearing a dark green divided riding skirt and a white blouse. Her blonde hair was still fixed in a single long braid which fell to the middle of her back. Jake wondered idly how long it was when unbound and spread. She skillfully guided the piebald horse she had hidden in the cottonwoods up the slope, keeping to the bank of the fast-flowing silver rill. Half of the time they were in the shade of the long row of Mexican palm trees. Reaching the point where he and Sarah had branched off onto the main road into the canyon on his last attempt, Christiana ignored the cut-off and continued on up the ever-steepening trail toward the rocky ridge above them.

'Are you sure this is the way?' Jake asked, as they paused in the heated shade of a stack of boulders to let their horses blow.

'I'm sure of nothing these days,' Christiana said. 'But yes, I think this is the way over the ridge. I've only been this far along once, with Sarah, but I think it is. She told me it was possible to make the ride.'

Jake could only hope it was. He took a drink of tepid water from his canteen and eyed the ridge uncertainly. Only row after row of huge jumbled boulders. High above them a single vulture glided past on motionless wings, sailing on the updraft. A little farther up the trail, Jake spotted a rough-skinned, black and orange Gila monster on a flat boulder, its glittering eyes fixed on them, its sides palpitating as it panted for air in the dry heat. Jake detoured around the great lizard as best he could — not that he thought the creature might leap at him and snap its powerful jaws into his flesh — they were incapable of jumping — but he disliked the very sight of the poisonous, primitive beast.

He found himself yearning for a place where there were no Gila monsters, sidewinders, scorpions or tarantulas, where a man could dress in the morning without having to shake out his boots to see what might have crawled into them overnight.

The sun continued to ride high, hot as a branding iron on Jake's back. He was perspiring freely: chest, back and arms. Christiana looked cooler, females not usually perspiring as freely as males, but her desert tan seemed to have paled. The horses were both laboring to find their way through the staggering collection of ancient boulders. Christiana pulled up again, swore and unreasonably slapped her horse's shoulder with the ends of her reins, causing the innocent piebald pony to flinch.

'I think I'm lost,' she said. 'We must have taken a wrong turn somewhere.' She put the back of her hand to her forehead. 'I really can't remember anymore!'

The voice beside them was calm, distant, familiar.

'Other way, Missie Chris — by broken pinyon tree.'

Jake, who had nearly drawn his Colt recognized the voice and now the form of Panda as he stepped toward them, his hand holding a gathered red kerchief with a few items bundled in it. The Yavapai Indian lifted a pointing finger.

'See the broken tree, burned tree? Find a small trail other side of it.'

Christiana's face relaxed with relief. Jake managed a tight smile. 'You're sure, Panda?'

'Very sure. I take that way to go home, I think.' He paused, shook his head slightly and then smiled at Jake. 'Bad days, huh?'

With that, the short Yavapai disappeared, his shadow seeming to merge with those of the boulders and then disappear into them.

'If Panda is leaving, things, must be bad back there,' Christiana said, turning her horse to follow the indicated trail. 'He was always satisfied to live here. Worthy did him a great favor at one time in the past, they say, though neither of them talked about it.'

'Kit's likely on a rampage,' Jake guessed. 'That would be a strong reason to move on.' Thinking about it, Jake considered, maybe the outlaw had good reason to be furious. Sarah had taken a large sum of money from him, and now his wife had fled. What if Kit discovered Jake with his wife? What would he assume about Jake and Christiana?

'If only Sarah had left well enough alone . . . ' Christiana said, but she never finished her remark. They rode on, and on, along the craggy hillside.

The sun was descending, but the day was no cooler when they reached the crest of the ridge. They had somehow managed to bypass the spring that fed the stream and so they had little water left for themselves and for the horses. No matter — they could look out across the high desert now. Somewhere in the distance lay Lewiston. Jake had made the ride before; he could make it again, assuming they could now find a way down through the rocks, but the path seemed much clearer on the north face, an easier ride by far than the road up had been.

The sandstorm was now only a desert memory. The sky held blue-white, clear and almost motionless. They made their way down onto the flats where spearlike yucca grew and passed an occasional tall ocotillo bush, the crimson flowers at their thorny tips now faded or blown away by the windstorm.

The land was flat; the day cooled; the

sun lowered its face and Christiana Blanchard rode along in high spirits. Then she darkened Jake's mood with a sour comment:

'What I said back there, Jake . . . I'm much afraid I really will have to kill Sarah. She's ruined my life, her father's life, and I doubt she cares a bit about it.'

Jake, weary and dry, did not respond. He only hoped that it was just talk. You hear things like that said all the time, but they're seldom acted upon. However, this wife of the outlaw Kit Blanchard had probably seen more arguments settled with violence than your average person, and might by now have adopted some of the outlaw ways herself. Jake had reason to hate Sarah himself, but he did not want her dead.

He thought a better alternative to shooting her might be to just give her the sound spanking she so obviously deserved.

They trailed into Lewiston at sundown. The western sky was colored red.

Blood-stained clouds hung lifelessly above the Arizona desert.

'I want to see the marshal,' Christiana Blanchard said as they walked their weary horses up the main street. 'Where can I find him?'

'All the way to the edge of town,' Jake said pointing the way. 'A low yellow-brick building. You'll see it. What did you need to talk to him about?'

'Why, Sarah of course! She stole from me.'

'Wasn't it Kit's money she took?'

'It was part mine! And the horse was mine! I'll get her for it.' The look in her eyes signaled deadly intent, but then she softened, smiled and asked, 'Don't you want to go to the marshal's office with me.'

'I'll be happy if I never see Trouffant again.' Jake had been fiddling with the badge on his shirt; now he unpinned it and handed it over to Christiana. 'Tell him I've resigned.'

'Where will you be going?' she asked with what seemed genuine interest.

'Nowhere far away for a time — my horse is beat down, I'm beat down. If they want to come and get me I'll make it easy on them.'

'I could buy you another horse,' Christiana said. 'I had some money of my own tucked away — a wise woman always does.'

'No thanks. Even with a fresh pony under me I wouldn't try to run. Anyway,' he added soberly, 'there's nowhere to go. I just want to see someone before they lock me up.'

'A girl,' Christina said.

'How did you know that?'

'Just by the way you said it. Look, Jake,' she said reaching into her saddlebags. 'Take a little money from me. Buy her a gift — whoever she is — women appreciate that,' and she slipped him a few coins which Jake didn't bother to look at or count. 'Good luck to you.'

'Thanks,' he replied, 'it looks like I'll be needing it.'

Then, immensely sure of herself, she

started her piebald horse forward, toward Marshal Trouffant's office. That was one trait she shared with her cousin Sarah — that utter confidence. Maybe it was bred into desert women. Jake watched her for a minute, then turned the weary buckskin away from town and headed north toward the little house where he hoped to find Cathy waiting.

Swinging down in front of the small white house, he caught a blur of movement to his right, glanced toward it and saw Chaser slinking away.

'What's the matter with you, dog?' Jake said in a low, stern voice. Chaser turned, wagged his tail indecisively, and for a moment it seemed that he would approach, but he turned and scooted away again.

The front door to the house opened.

Cathy stood in the doorway, her slender figure silhouetted against the vague lantern light behind her. Her almost-curly brown hair was unpinned and in near disarray. She clutched a robe to her throat, lifted one hand toward Jake and spoke.

'Oh! I thought I heard a man speaking . . . and I thought it was you. I just didn't dare hope — you made it back.'

'I made it back,' Jake said stepping up onto the sagging porch, surprised at how much he seemed to tower over the small woman. 'I don't figure they'll let me run around free for long, though. There's too many people holding grudges against me.'

'Come in,' she said taking his hand. 'Come in and tell me what happened. All about it. Did the sandstorm change things for you? We saw it here in Lewiston, but it was far to the east. I could tell it was bad, and I knew you were out there . . .

'Come sit down. Tell me what happened and what is going to happen now.'

'Aren't your friends home?' he asked

'They'll be off work in a little while. Not just yet.' She patted her unruly hair uncertainly, realized that she was only partially dressed, seemed to shrug that off as unimportant and continued, speaking rapidly.

'I'll get you some coffee. Sit at the table.'

'It's still warm to start a fire in the stove.'

'That's not important — the day will start cooling off soon, as you know. I'll just open the back door and start the pot boiling. And I suppose I'd better pull on some other clothes!' she added sheepishly.

'If you like,' Jake agreed. He hadn't even really thought of how she was dressed, how her hair was fixed. It seemed kind of cozy and comforting to have a woman in her natural state bustling about, eager to be helpful, but he supposed she had to consider maintaining some sort of propriety, especially with her housemates due home soon.

She bustled off toward a back room leaving Jake to sit watching the glow of the fire behind the grill of the black iron stove. Beyond the open door he could see the first stars blinking across the clear twilight sky. There was a scrabbling sound on the back porch and Jake didn't even lift his head as he called out, 'Well come in or don't, you dumb mutt!'

Chaser, who might have been considering trying to sneak into the house, turned tail and vanished. Making himself more at home than was probably correct, Jake rose and walked to the cooler in the corner of the room, opened the narrow wooden door, and, using his belt knife, cut a large piece of fat and skin from the ham there. He tossed the meat out onto the porch, listened to more scrabbling and the dog's low-throated question, returned to the table and sat down wearily, smelling the coffee which had begun to boil on the stove.

He was beat down. That's what he had told Christiana Blanchard, and it was the truth. He hadn't realized just how exhausted he was until now. He could have put his head down on the table and fallen asleep in an instant. How had he ever gotten himself into this, and how long could it go on?

Even if Marshal Trouffant was willing to let matters rest, Sarah would not be — in her mind she had made a devil's bargain with Jake to kill or capture Kit Blanchard, and he had failed her. Even without Sarah, there was Hutch Gleason to consider. He must be thinking that Jake had slipped away from them on the desert for some devious reason of his own, and when he learned that Jake had returned with Christiana Blanchard, he would be sure of it.

Then there was the stolen buckskin horse and Bert Stiles. Would Stiles be willing to expend the time and resources to track Jake down? Who knew? Stiles nursed a grudge well. Cathy came back into the kitchen.

She had hastily brushed her hair and seemed to have splashed some sort of powder on. She wore a neat little yellow dress with a thin piece of lace around the neckline. Jake smiled at her, trying to tell her in unspoken language that he appreciated the effort she had made. What he said was:

'Doesn't anyone ever feed that dog!'

Cathy laughed. Glancing that way as she reached for the handle of the big blue coffee pot, a towel in her hand for a hot pad, she saw Chaser chewing on the slice of ham skin. At her look, the dog snatched up what it had not eaten and raced away, toenails clicking across the porch.

'Oh, he eats well enough,' Cathy answered. 'What he's after,' she said, pouring coffee into two white ceramic cups, 'is something a little more satisfying. He's hungry for companionship but has forgotten how to go about finding it.'

'No sugar,' Jake pled. He looked to where Chaser had vanished into the night and thought about what Cathy had said. Poor Chaser, poor everybody.

He spent the next half hour telling

Cathy what had happened out on the desert. She listened quietly, her eyes filled with concern and deep thoughtfulness. When he had finally finished she rose, went to the small kitchen window and looked out at the starfields in the long sky. The moon had just begun to rise and it touched the tips of the cottonwood trees beyond the yard with soft gold. Without turning back toward Jake she said quietly:

'I wonder what happened to that Indian man, the one name Panda that you mentioned.'

'I don't know,' Jake told her. 'Maybe he decided to try going home to his people, though I was told he was not welcome there. Or maybe he is doomed to wander the desert alone forever.'

Like so many others, it seemed: Poor Panda, poor Sarah, poor Cathy, poor Chaser.

Poor Jake Staggs.

'You must be hungry,' Cathy said now as she turned toward him and brightened his small world with a smile.

'I don't really have much around to cook for you just now, but if you'll come by the restaurant in the morning, I'll see that you're fixed up.' She hesitated. 'That is, if you are still going to be here in the morning.'

'I'll still be here, Cathy. There's nowhere left to run. I'm at the end of my trail, and I know it.'

8

Twilight was settling by the time Hutch Gleason came within sight of Lewiston again. His horse was dragging and his mood was sour. Only two men rode with him: the red-headed Fulton brothers — Champ and Engle. They were two of his regular hands on the Cat's Cradle Ranch up north and had no choice but to stick with their boss if they were going to continue to collect their wages. The other men, volunteers in the posse hoping for a big payday, had quit him.

When the sandstorm had cleared Hutch had not seen Jake Staggs, but then he had known that he wouldn't. The bastard had taken advantage of the savagely blowing sand's cover to slip off into Smuggler's Gulch. Hutch thought that he had been right all along — Staggs was one of the horse thieves himself.

There had been no point in going on, Hutch knew. Without provisions and water, they might as well start chasing ghosts as try to find and track Kit Blanchard in that vast expanse of harsh land. He didn't even argue with the men who wanted to quit the posse, disperse and head for home. There was no argument to be made.

Now as twilight settled and the western sky flushed to a lavender shade, Hutch saw Champ Fulton stand in his stirrups and point to the north.

'It's him, Mr. Gleason! It's him.' Hutch let his eyes follow the pointing finger and finally he was able to make out the two shadowy figures of men on horseback riding in the direction of Lewiston. 'That is Kit Blanchard!' Champ shouted. 'I recognize that paint horse he favors.'

Gleason was not so sure; the light was poor. But he, too, knew that Kit Blanchard rode a leggy paint pony — they had pursued him riding that horse the week before.

'It's him all right,' Engle Fulton chimed in. 'Besides, who else would be riding way out here?'

Gleason still was not sure, but he trusted their younger eyes and without answering, touched heels to the red roan he was riding and urged the weary animal to make speed: no easy task for a dehydrated, tired animal across the sandy flats. Gleason's hat blew off and he let it go. Hutch was leaning across his dun horse's withers, trying to goad his own mount to speed. The red-headed brothers were eager and animated. No wonder.

If Hutch Gleason was mainly concerned about revenge, paying Kit back for stealing his blooded horses, to the young men the reward money that had enticed them out onto the desert was paramount. The five thousand dollars on Kit Blanchard's head did not now have to be divided up among the members of a twelve-man posse. It was a fortune to men of their ages and background.

There were only two outlaws ahead. Who the other one man might be was open to conjecture. Hutch considered that he couldn't be so lucky as to have it turn out to be Jake Staggs. That would be too much to hope for, but whoever the other man was, he probably also had a price on his head, had probably been among the bandits who had raided the Cat's Cradle and made off with his Kentucky horses.

Sundown flared briefly in the west. Gold splashed against the pale pink and crimson of the sky. They were gaining on the horse thieves who still seemed unaware of the pursuit. Hutch's horse was faltering under him; he only prayed that it could find enough stamina to stay the chase. The outlaws disappeared into deep shadow; they had dipped into a shallow ravine. Hutch cursed silently, but then the riders emerged again and there was still enough remaining light to make out the paint pony.

The outlaws touched spurs to their

horses' flanks and the animals leaped into a run.

'They seen us!' Engle yelled unnecessarily. The outlaws' horses seemed to be much fresher than their own. Hutch unlimbered his Winchester rifle. They were not faster than a .44-40 slug.

The outlaws now split up; the man on the dun pony breaking off toward the east, Kit Blanchard on his paint lining it out toward Lewiston.

'Forget about the other one! We're taking Kit Blanchard down!' Gleason cried out, gathering his reins in one hand as he shouldered his rifle and fired three times in rapid succession.

With a whoop Engle raised his own rifle and levered through half a dozen rounds. Champ Fulton's rifle barked as well. The paint was gaining ground, but one among the barrage of bullets, either by luck or chance, caught the pony and as they watched, it stumbled and rolled, its rider flung free to lie motionless against the desert floor.

'Got him!' Engle exulted and they

raced on, flogging their mounts with the ends of their reins. If their horses foundered now, what did it matter? They would have enough gold to buy fifty more horses.

Slowing, they cautiously approached the fallen paint horse, walking their exhausted horses.

'Where is he?' Engle hissed uneasily. 'I can't see him.'

'Stay alert boys. The man can shoot.' Hutch Gleason, who thought himself to be nerveless, now glanced around anxiously, his rifle gripped tightly in his hands. The shadows were deep and long, the sky darkening. If they lost Kit Blanchard now . . .

'There he is!' Champ shouted out and they now could see a man sitting on the sand beneath a thorny mesquite, the stars casting a lacy pattern of shadows across his face and arms.

'That's not him!' Engle said as they approached. Hutch Gleason and Champ Fulton swung down while Engle held their reins. 'Who is he?'

From the shadows a middle-aged man with a craggy face, his blond hair sprayed across a nearly bald head looked up at them. He was holding his ribs and it seemed difficult for him to speak, but he smiled up at them and told them:

'Kit's going to be almighty sore with you boys — that was his favorite horse,' Will Sizemore said.

'How the hell . . . ?' Engle asked.

'They switched horses when they were down in the gully back there,' his brother said, scowling at Will Sizemore as he spoke. 'What's your name?' he asked, still hopeful of claiming some reward money.

'Sizemore,' Will said, 'but there's no paper out on me, men. You've wasted your time.'

'That's what he would say,' Champ Fulton said. 'He's one of them, though, isn't he, Mr. Gleason? One of the horse thieves. He must be. He was riding with Kit Blanchard.'

'I was riding with him,' Will lied, 'but

I just kind of fell in with him along the trail. I didn't have any idea who he was at first. He flashed a gun and made me change horses with him. That's no crime, boys.'

Hutch Gleason was furious. Only minutes ago he had believed that he had caught Kit Blanchard; now he felt like a fool. He raised a hand as if to strike Will Sizemore, realized the futility of it and lowered his hand again.

'What'll we do with him?' Champ Fulton asked.

'We'll take him along to town. Maybe the marshal knows something about who he is and if there's money on his head.'

'Who's he going to ride with?' Engle asked anxiously. With the promise of the reward money slipping away he realized that the horse he rode was nearly the only asset he had in the world. It had already been sorely used and he did not want it to be forced to carry double.

'He'll have to walk it,' Gleason said

coldly. 'Can't be more than five or ten miles. Help him up, Champ.'

Champ Fulton bent down, made sure that Sizemore had no belt gun and hoisted him to his feet. Well, it was just more bad luck, Champ was thinking as Sizemore stood there holding his ribs. Champ could have just shrugged it all off as a mistake if Will Sizemore, planting his recovered hat on his head, hadn't stood there grinning at them.

★   ★   ★

At least he had had a good breakfast, Jake Staggs thought as he stood in front of the restaurant looking out across the town at the long blue-white desert and toward the chocolate mountains beyond. It might be a while before he saw any of this again. The long night had given birth to a bitter decision just before dawn. He had told Cathy as he waited at the breakfast table:

'I'm just going to turn myself in and get it over with.'

'Turn yourself in for what!' Cathy asked. She had greeted him with a pretty smile. Now her lips went tight and her face went ashen. She swayed slightly on her feet. She ignored the other customers trying to get her attention.

'For whatever they want to charge me with. I can't go on like this any longer, Cathy. It's worse than any prison could be.'

Jake Staggs strode heavily, but not reluctantly toward the marshal's office, the low morning sun in his eyes. He felt that he was carrying all the debris of a misspent life on his shoulders. He had to find a way to unburden himself, to start over. He was thinking, he realized, not with a shock but with a sort of awakening feeling, that he was thinking of starting over again with Cathy.

Billy Bostwick was behind the marshal's desk, boots propped up, laboring through what seemed to be the same newspaper. He lifted curious eyes to

Jake, folded the paper and placed it aside.

'What is it, Staggs?'

'I want to see the marshal.'

'I don't think he's able to see anyone right now. He's taken a turn for the worse. I think it's those two women that caused it,' he confided.

'Sarah and Christiana?'

'Those two,' Bostwick said with a nod. 'The one badgering him about her reward money, the other wanting her sister, or what is she . . . ?'

'Her cousin.'

'She wanting her cousin arrested for theft. They nattered and demanded until twice I had to throw one of them out and the marshal, he says, don't ever let those females around him again.'

'Where are they now?'

'I don't know and I don't care,' Bostwick said defiantly. 'Now what is it you wanted, Staggs?'

'To turn myself in and clear all of this up.'

Bostwick looked deeply puzzled.

'What is it you wanted to turn yourself in for exactly?'

'The horse I'm riding is stolen, for one thing.'

Bostwick scratched his ear and nodded. 'How did you happen to come by it?'

'The man I was working for refused to pay me.'

'So you took a horse instead?'

'That's about it, but that's made me a wanted man.'

'I never seen any paper on you,' Bostwick said. 'To me it seems like you might have had the right to take your payment where you could. 'Course I'm not a judge — I have no idea how the law reads in a case like this.' Bostwick leaned forward and folded his hands together on the desk.

'I don't know what to tell you — the marshal's the only one who can decide whether it's proper to lock you up, and without a warrant . . . We'll just have to wait and see what he says when he's able.'

'It's Hutch Gleason that was making the complaint.'

'Hutch Gleason is a puffed-up, bullying old fool. Besides he didn't say anything to me last night.'

'He's back?'

'He is,' Bostwick said. 'He's the one who brought the new prisoner in.'

'New . . . ?' Jake turned toward the cells, one of which had a somehow-familiar man sitting on the chain-supported wooden bunk, watching and listening. It was Will Sizemore.

'Do you know that man?' Bostwick asked.

'I'm not sure.'

'Hutch Gleason said he was a Kit Blanchard rider. The prisoner,' he nodded toward the cell, 'says he just happened to fall in with Kit along the trail. You were never part of that gang, were you, Staggs?'

'I told you I was not. Would Marshal Trouffant have made me a deputy if he thought I was?'

'I don't suppose he would have,' Billy

Bostwick answered slowly. 'To tell you the truth, this is all too much for me, Staggs. Anything else you want to turn yourself in for?'

'There's the shooting of Eduardo Blanco,' Jake said, and Bostwick listened and nodded as if taking mental notes, 'and the deaths of Lemon Jack and River Tremaine.' The deputy held up a hand to silence him.

'Look, Staggs, Lemon Jack Baker and River Tremaine were well known horse thieves. In Blanco's case — well we've got a few witnesses who say that he goaded you into the fight and drew first. As far as the other two are concerned well, we've got only that Sarah Worthy's word for what happened, but she was eager enough to claim the reward in the first place, and she says the men you shot were outlaws with a price on their heads.'

'So was Blanco, but still, Hutch Gleason and Trouffant both said I could be tried for the killings. The girl, Sarah, threatened to back up the tale that I was a Kit Blanchard rider and a killer at that.' Jake was growing frustrated. He had never known that it was so difficult to get yourself arrested.

And suddenly it no longer seemed like such a great idea. Bostwick explained patiently:

'Even if that's so,' he said, 'I remember when the marshal gave you a badge. I recall, too, that he said he was making the assignment retroactive. Again, I'm no judge — wouldn't want to be — but how can you stand trial for following your oath of office and taking down three known outlaws?

'That's just me personally, you understand. I don't know what Trouffant will want to do.' Bostwick stood, stretched and said, 'But as for me, I can't lock you up for what don't seem to be crimes.

'Sam Trouffant,' Bostwick added with mingled guilt and pleasure, 'only went along with the woman because he was thinking about retirement and how little a crippled man could do to support himself. Now Sam doesn't feel like he's going to make it. And he wants nothing more to do with that Sarah Worthy. So go some place else to unburden yourself, Staggs. Maybe you could find a priest to talk to. The law's got no hold on you as of now.'

'Can I talk to the prisoner?' Jake inquired, nodding toward the cell where Will Sizemore sat, half-smiling.

'I don't see why not,' the deputy answered with a shrug. 'He's another man we've got no evidence against. He's locked up on Hutch Gleason's say-so. I don't think we'll be able to hold him more than overnight unless some paper on him shows up. But, not to repeat myself, these are decisions that Marshal Trouffant will have to make.'

Jake walked toward the cell, and, keeping his voice low, said, 'Hello, Sizemore.' The outlaw didn't rise from his bunk. He put his hands to his mouth and answered in a muffled voice.

'Hello, Jake. I didn't expect to see

163

you again. Was I you, I would have been long gone down the trail.'

'Things didn't work out that simply.'

'They never do.'

'Where's Kit?'

Sizemore's hands fell away from his face and he smiled. 'Are you going to go after him?'

'I'd probably just try to make sure I didn't go anywhere near him, wherever he was.'

'A smart man would — he's got a grudge against you. But I don't know where he is, Jake.'

'Looking for the women, do you think?' Jake asked.

'I would imagine, wouldn't you? He's around somewhere. They found my dun horse that he was riding roaming loose.'

'What happened to the gang?' Jake wanted to know.

Sizemore frowned. 'The Mexican didn't want to meet the price Kit was asking for the horses. Oh, he wanted them right enough, he just didn't want to pay for them. There was a dust-up. Kit shot a man and the Mexicans got two of ours. Kit kept the boys with him afterward, promising he'd pay them out of what he had stashed back home. Only the money was gone. Christiana was gone. You and Sarah were gone. Someone had killed Lemon Jack and River Tremaine. Our horse herd was gone, stolen by the Mexicans, and we didn't even have hay for our own mounts — that's usually thrown in as part of the deal when we bargain with the Mexicans. The boys wouldn't stand for not being paid, though Kit told them we'd make it up on the next raid. They started to mutter and then to drift away one by one or in pairs.'

'I see,' Jake said thoughtfully. 'What about Worthy?'

'To tell you the truth, if it weren't for missing Sarah, I think the old man is relieved that it all happened. He was tired of the canyon being used as an outlaw camp, though I guess Kit paid him well enough. He's probably got enough coins tucked away to make out comfortably the rest of his days.'

'The deputy says they'll probably have to cut you loose tomorrow,' Jake told Sizemore.

'I heard that. I hope they do, because I know Kit Blanchard better than most men. If he thinks they're going to hang me, he'll find a way to bust me out, and wherever Kit goes, there'll be a trail of blood behind him.'

Bostwick called to them, 'That's enough time!'

'All right,' Jake hollered back. 'Good luck to you, Sizemore,' he said, and the two men shook hands.

'The same to you, Jake. Remember though, we're on opposite sides of the table — Kit Blanchard will take care of me, but he has a grudge against you for helping the women and for killing three of his men. If he sees you, he'll take care of you, too. In a totally different way.'

'I'll be careful.'

'Jake, if I was you, I'd get out of here.

Because you'll never again take a step without feeling the need to glance back over your shoulder. Kit Blanchard has a way of getting things done.'

★   ★   ★

Jake went out onto the plankwalk in front of the jail, tugging his hat low against the morning sun. It was warm and pleasant, but that was the way the desert had of warning that by noon it would be searing hot across the land. He trudged back toward the restaurant. Cathy had been very depressed when he saw her last. Maybe seeing that he was still a free man — for now — would bring a smile back to her lips. There was no lightness in Jake's heart as he clomped along the plankwalk. Talking to Billy Bostwick had helped a little, but he still had a few deep concerns, namely Sarah Worthy, Hutch Gleason and Kit Blanchard, each of whom might be nursing a deadly grudge against him for their own reasons. He was hardly cheerful when he re-entered the restaurant through the white door, but he put on a smile for Cathy's sake when he saw her looking at him across the room. He sat at what had become his usual table and waited for her, watching the pale sky through the two large windows.

She came with coffee and bent low, 'Is everything straightened out now?' she asked hopefully.

'Well, they didn't want to lock me up,' Staggs said easily. She could read the concern in his eyes if not in his manner. 'Not yet,' he felt compelled to add.

'Then you can leave. Just ride out.'

'I haven't got a horse,' he reminded her. 'Even if I resorted to stealing the buckskin again, he's not fit for the long trail.' He looked deeply into her eyes and said, 'Besides I still don't have a place to ride to. Cathy, have you seen those women in here this morning? You know who I mean.'

'Both of them. Not at the same time,

thankfully. The dark haired one — she's Sarah Worthy, right? — came in for toast and tea very early. She kept her eyes moving, searching the room and everyone who came in.'

'And the blonde, Christiana?'

'She came in not half an hour ago. She wanted her breakfast in a box — she said she felt like eating it in her room.'

'What kind of breakfast was it?'

'What kind?' Cathy was puzzled by the question. 'Fried potatoes, three eggs, sausage and ham.'

'That's a lot of breakfast for a small woman,' Jake commented thoughtfully.

'Well, I've seen a few small women in here eat more than you'd think they could handle.' She studied him again, her brown eyes searching. 'What are you thinking, Jake?'

'I'm thinking that Kit Blanchard is in town, that somehow he and his wife have made up. They share a common cause, after all. Kit Blanchard wants his treasury money back and he knows who has it — Sarah. As for Christiana . . . I'm beginning to believe her when she says that she wants her cousin dead.'

'Then all three of them are staying at the hotel?' Cathy asked.

'It seems like it,' Jake said, pushing his chair back to rise from the table.

'Jake, don't do it!' Cathy gripped his arm with her small hand. A few heads turned their way. 'Whatever you are thinking, don't do it,' she said in a lower, more insistent voice.

'I have to, Cathy. Don't you understand? Those three are at the root of all of my problems. There has to be a resolution.'

'I can get Billy Bostwick — if I tell him that Kit Blanchard is in town, he'll come soon enough.'

'Will he?' Jake didn't think so. Billy was a careful, methodical man. He would want to know what evidence they had. None. But Jake knew in his heart that the leader of the Smuggler's Gulch gang was out there waiting, and he thought he knew where.

'It's better that I go after him now than wait until he comes after me,' Jake said, firmly, removing Cathy's fingers from his arm.

He thought of taking Cathy's advice as he trudged across the dusty street through the growing heat of the day and made his way toward the Lewiston Hotel. The girl was right, of course — let those three settle matters among themselves. It was really none of his business. He could simply keep his head down and bide his time until he was sure they had cleared out of town.

He had nearly convinced himself to do just that when he approached the front door to the hotel to find Sarah Worthy in a white dress with pale green trimming standing talking animatedly to Hutch Gleason.

Gleason glanced at Jake as he stepped up onto the boardwalk, said something to Sarah and then turned away, his face smug. What sort of deal had the woman made this time? She had tried using Jake Staggs to find and kill Kit. Then she had fastened onto the notion of using Sam Trouffant.

It looked now as if she had made a bargain with Hutch Gleason to kill Kit Blanchard. Perhaps they meant to split the reward, perhaps not. Gleason was still angry enough over the loss of his Kentucky-bred horses to kill Kit out of hand. And Jake knew by the smile on the dark-eyed girl's lips as he walked toward the hotel doorway that she had somehow discovered where Kit was and informed Hutch.

He knew that just as surely as he knew that more than one man or woman was doomed to die on this day.

9

Sarah turned at the sound of his approaching boots and looked flustered for only a brief second. Then she smiled and greeted him with, 'Why, Mister Staggs, it's good to see you again. Fine morning, isn't it?'

'It was.' He started to ease past her but she blocked his way, looking up at him with those dark eyes which could not conceal the venom she was harboring inside.

'Will you buy me tea somewhere?' she asked, leaning close to him. Her smile was still in place, but her hands were clenched tightly.

'Maybe some other time,' Jake said, pushing past her.

'Where are you going?' she asked, her voice now taut with stress.

'I still have a room in the hotel. I'm going to it.'

'Why?' she said with uncontrolled excitement.

'Because it's my room,' Jake said evenly, 'and I feel like going up to it.'

Her body was now rigid, her eyes flashing; there was no sign of a smile on her face. 'Don't you interfere!' she shouted. 'Don't you dare interfere!'

'I won't, not unless I have to.'

'I'll call the marshal,' Sarah threatened as he turned his back to her and started across the hotel lobby. 'I'll see you hanged! I'll . . . ' Either she could think of no more threats or her anger had strangled off her voice. She said nothing else but, lifting her skirts, she chased after Jake as he made his way toward the staircase.

'What room are they in?' he asked over his shoulder as he mounted the stairs.

'I don't have to tell you!'

'It doesn't matter. I'll be able to find it when the shooting starts.'

She gave a muffled little shriek and started after him. It didn't take long to find the right room. Jake saw a man lurking in the shadows beside the door to one of the rooms but before he could approach, the prowling man shouldered the door open and entered, gun drawn. By the light from the room's window, Jake could make out the heavy features of Hutch Gleason, and he rushed towards him, drawing his own Colt.

Before Jake could reach the open door two shots rang out, their echo rolling down the enclosed hallway, and black powder smoke rolled from the room. Jake slowed his headlong rush and peered cautiously around the corner. Hutch Gleason lay crumpled against the hardwood floor and by the window stood Kit Blanchard, his gun smoking. Christiana was standing beside Kit and she clutched at his arm, but Kit shoved her aside, stepped over the window sill and dropped to the ground before Jake could stop him. Christiana, hearing Jake's boot-heels against the floor, whirled toward him.

'Stop where you are!' she ordered.

She was holding a small silver pistol in her hand. Her eyes were frantic, her hand trembled, but she looked as ready to fight as a cornered she-wolf. Jake halted in his tracks, standing near the bulky body of the fallen Hutch Gleason.

'The fat fool thought he could take Kit Blanchard!' Christiana said with a proud toss of her head. Those eyes which had been fixed on Jake now shifted to the doorway and Jake had a sinking feeling that he knew what had happened: Sarah Worthy had followed him into the room. Christiana's blue eyes went as cold as ice.

'You ruined everything!' Christiana screamed, and then pulled the trigger and the little silver gun sent a bullet flying past Jake's ear. It struck Sarah Worthy full in the chest and a crimson stain spread across the white bodice of her dress.

Sarah stretched out both arms, opened her mouth and collapsed, dead before she hit the floor. Jake flinched and raised his own gun, but the pistol in Christiana's hand never shifted his way. She stood holding the smoking gun loosely at her side, her other hand to her breast. She took a step back, dropped the pistol which clattered to the floor, and sagged onto the bed behind her.

There were bootsteps rushing down the corridor toward the room. A man cried out. Jake went to the window, and after one glance out to make sure that Kit Blanchard was not there waiting, stepped over the sill and leaped from the ledge to the alley below.

Which way? He did not think the outlaw would run toward Main Street and all of the citizens there, so he turned away from town, running up the narrow alley with his gun gripped tightly in his hand.

He did not want to kill Kit Blanchard. He did not want to have to get into a shootout with the savage outlaw leader. But he wanted to end it. It had to all end sometime, and it seemed that killing Kit Blanchard was the only way to finish everything.

Of course having Kit Blanchard kill him would effectively end it all as well.

Sarah was gone now; the marshal probably dying and Hutch Gleason would trouble him no longer. Only Kit Blanchard remained, and the badman would be a threat to him and any hopes for future happiness so long as he lived. Jake ran on determinedly, but with a faltering sense of confidence. Kit Blanchard was plain dangerous, and he knew it. Yet there was no one else to call on, no one to rely on. Within minutes Kit could be out on the desert, and in time he would reform his gang and remember that — in his own mind at least — Jake Staggs was partly to blame for his misfortunes.

On the desert. Of course that was where Kit would be headed. Where any pursuit could be seen, where he knew every track and arroyo, and then would he try to make his way back to Smuggler's Gulch?

Why would he not? It had always been a place of safety, his refuge against the world, unknown to most, hidden and secure. That was where he would head; Jake was certain of it. He slowed his pace, looked around at the mouth of the alley, the willow-clotted, dry creek-bed beyond and holstered his pistol. He retraced his path, going past the hotel and saw two men looking out of Christiana's window. One of them called to Jake, but he ignored him. On the main street spectators were gathering in front of the hotel. In passing, he heard someone say that Kit Blanchard was dead. Another excited man said that Blanchard had just gunned down three men and that they had him cornered upstairs.

Jake trudged on, head down as the sun beat against his back and shoulders. He made his way to the stable and went into the musty smelling, shadowed building to find the buckskin eyeing him dolefully. The horse had no need to worry. The buckskin was too used up for the ride Jake had in mind.

'Help you?' the stableman asked. He was narrow, had a game leg and frightened eyes.

'I want that dun horse saddled,' Jake said, pointing at Will Sizemore's pony.

'That horse . . . ' the man objected.

'That horse was being ridden by an outlaw. It belongs to the town of Lewiston now. I am a deputy marshal. My name's Jake Staggs. You can ask Sam Trouffant or Billy Bostwick.'

The man looked doubtful. He glanced at Jake's shirt front, saw no badge but proceeded to saddle Will Sizemore's dun horse. The stableman was not the sort to seek out trouble, and besides, it was not his own mount that he was giving away.

In fifteen minutes, Jake Staggs was back on the desert, bee-lining it south toward Smuggler's Gulch. Jake saw no other rider across the long desert flats, but Kit Blanchard knew the secret ways of the land, its gullies and ridges and hidden trails, and he did not doubt that the outlaw was capable of making his way to the robbers' roost nearly unseen. Perhaps, Jake thought, he had guessed wrong and Blanchard had chosen not to head this way, even though it was the only destination that made sense.

It was high noon with the white sun hanging motionless in a desolate sky when Jake came upon the rocky bluffs guarding the entrance to Smuggler's Gulch. He drew up the dun and let it blow as he considered — which way? From what Will Sizemore had told him it seemed unlikely that there were enough men remaining in the outlaw band to post sentries among the boulders, but that did not mean that Kit Blanchard himself, being a cautious man by nature, was not positioned somewhere among the rocks with a long gun.

Jake didn't have the energy to try the ridge route he had ridden with Christiana again, and it was punishing for a horse. He decided on the old Indian cut-off that he and Sarah had used when he had made his first escape from the canyon. It was a guessing game, of course — with Kit Blanchard you never knew, but the man could not be everywhere at once.

Cautiously then, Jake made his way up among the boulders as the sun continued to beat mercilessly down. He found the foot of the Indian trail fairly easily and followed its winding path through the scrambled rocks. Now he rode with his rifle — Will Sizemore's actually; it had been left in his saddle scabbard — in his hand, his eyes darting from point to uncertain point. A rabbit skittered away before the dun's hoofs startled him as did the slithering exit of a desert rattler from the trail. He was jumpy, he knew it, and could do nothing about it.

Cresting the trail near where he and Sarah had been ambushed by Lemon Jack Baker and River Tremaine, he drew up the wearying dun horse to let it blow and to study the land below him. He knew the layout of the place well enough by now — the long row of Mexican fan palms following the course of the creek, the cottonwood trees below hiding the ranch house and horse pens. He could see the main road leading into and out of the gorge, but he saw no one moving across the land, heard nothing but the whispering of the dry desert wind as it wove its way among the boulders and ruffled the fronds of the palm trees. That did not make him feel any safer.

True, Kit Blanchard could have made a different decision — ridden off to some outlaw camp known only to him, but Jake did not think it likely. This was his sanctuary, and if he decided to start his horse stealing ring again, he would need the security of the hidden gorge.

No, Kit was down there somewhere, Jake thought, his mouth tightening. He took a sip of tepid water from his canteen and gave matters some thought. Eventually he decided to hold off until sundown before he tried to make his way down to the house. In darkness he would have less chance of being seen; by then Kit Blanchard might have lowered his guard slightly, believing that he had not been followed.

Perhaps that was all only hopeful conjecture, but Jake had made his decision, so he swung down from the dun, loosened its saddle cinches slightly and let it poke around for sparse graze.

He waited.

It seemed like days, years, before the glaring white sun finally decided that it was growing weary and heeled over toward the western mountains; days, years more before it began to color, turning deep yellow and then red as purple evening settled. Jake watched the doves heading home again, saw the first owl of the evening rise into the sundown sky on broad, heavy wings. With a sigh and an dull ache in the pit of his stomach he rose, tightened the dun's cinches again and heeled it forward into the depths of Smuggler's Gulch.

He couldn't trust himself to find his

way in full darkness, so there was still a hint of color, a faint light in the western sky, but the canyon was already deep in shadow, and as he reached the bottom where the Indian trail intersected the main road, the world seemed to have gone suddenly dark. He could not read the sign the passing horses had left in the earth well enough to tell if any one of them was newer than the others. So many horses had passed that way in recent days.

There had to be a moon somewhere in the sky, but it was low and the gorge cut off any light it may have been casting. In near total darkness Jake walked his horse toward Worthy's house, accompanied by the silence. Frogs grumbled along the creek, but they too fell silent as he approached and then passed them by.

There was a light in the window of the stone house. That was not surprising, really; Jake had been told that Worthy meant to stay in the canyon no matter what. He was yet another man with no place else to go. Jake steered his pony away from the road and into the cottonwood grove. He meant to approach the house on foot. The horse's plodding hoofs were loud in the night and who knew if the animal might choose to nicker at the wrong moment.

He dropped the reins to the dun, leaving it to manage on its own and he slipped through the shadows. Starlight now began to flicker through the upper reaches of the trees. Not quite enough light to see, and hopefully not enough to be seen by. Jake had left his long gun in its scabbard. This figured to call for close work, and he carried his Colt low and solidly in his hand. He crept toward the back corner of the house where he again paused to listen. There were no voices from within, leading him to believe that Worthy was alone. Of course, as he had witnessed, Kit and Worthy were not given to much conversation. He waited, but there was going to be nothing learned from standing alone in the night, and he knew that he was only trying to postpone the inevitable. All he could do was be as ready as possible and hope for the best.

He eased around to the front of the house and stepped up onto the sagging plank porch, cursing silently as one of the boards creaked under his tread, a sound which seemed unnaturally loud in the utter stillness of the dark night. Surely that sound had not been loud enough to hear behind the stone wall of the house, he convinced himself. But a man can always be wrong.

Jake took one more step and found out how wrong he had been. His senses on full alert, his nerves taut and ready, Kit Blanchard had heard the small noise, and he now flung open the cabin door, his gun leveled.

'Thought I'd be meeting you again,' Kit Blanchard snarled.

'Who is it!' The voice belonged to Worthy, and Jake glanced toward the interior of the house to see the little round man approaching, shotgun in his hands. Kit did not glance at him. His gaze was steady, unwavering, as if challenging Jake Staggs to make a move.

'Just Staggs,' Kit said in a low growl.

'Jake? What's he want here?' Worthy asked. The stubby little man held back a few steps, peering toward the doorway. It must have been hard to make out Jake's face in the darkness, but finally he seemed to recognize him. 'Well, hello Jake.' Then he asked anxiously:

'Where's Sarah?' he looked hopefully beyond Jake into the empty darkness.

'She's dead,' Jake had to tell him.

'Dead?' the man's eyes glassed over for a minute. He was stunned, staggered by the news. 'What happened to her? Was it . . . ?' he looked at Kit Blanchard who now glanced at him long enough to snarl, 'It wasn't me, you old fool. I didn't even know about it until just this minute.'

'Then who . . . ?' Worthy asked Jake.

'It was Christiana,' Jake said. 'She

shot her cousin.'

The news had an impact on Worthy and on Kit who seemed genuinely astonished.

'I'll be damned,' Kit Blanchard said. 'She meant what she was saying.'

Worthy was crushed. His daughter dead, his niece guilty of the killing. His wrath settled on Kit Blanchard. 'This is all your fault, damn you Kit! All of it. You've poisoned everything and everyone since the day you rode onto my land.'

'Quit blathering, you old fool,' Kit commanded.

Worthy shot him.

The shotgun erupted with the roar of a small cannon in the confines of the house. There was a brief spurt of flame from the twin muzzles of the twelve-gauge and the whining sound of buckshot striking the stone walls. The double-ought pellets that hit Kit Blanchard produced a thumping sound like a butcher's cleaver striking meat, and Kit pitched forward on his face, his pistol clattering free of his hand.

'I should have done that years ago,' Worthy said, but he said it unsteadily, and Jake saw that his knees were trembling, his face bloodless as he made his way to a rocking chair in the corner and sagged onto it.

'Is there anyone else around?' Jake asked urgently.

'No, no one's going to come running. They're all gone, cleared out.' Worthy lifted pouched eyes to Jake, 'Do you suppose they'll hang me for this?'

'It's more likely they'll give you a reward.'

'I don't want any damn reward!' Worthy yelled. 'I want my daughter back!'

After a minute, Worthy's face returned to its natural color and he was less shaky, less agitated when he asked Jake, 'Will you do something for me? Will you take him out of here, Jake? I don't want to see Kit Blanchard again even if it's as I'm throwing him into his grave.'

10

By moonlight, Jake made his way up the road toward the desert flats. Kit Blanchard's body was draped over the back of the outlaw's own horse. Or, as Worthy had said, 'Someone's horse. Kit Blanchard never paid for a horse he was riding in his life.'

The thing that worried Worthy the most, of course, was what would become of Christiana, though he expressed no wish to ever see her again if she had killed Sarah. Jake thought he had an idea about that.

'Sarah was killed in Christiana's hotel room while Kit was shooting it out with Hutch Gleason. It seems to me that it's most likely she was caught in a crossfire. I'll have to talk to Christiana. If she's willing to go along with that story, they'll probably set her free.'

'Will the law accept that explanation?' Worthy asked, frowning.

'From what I know of the law in Lewiston,' Jake told him, 'they'll accept almost anything that makes their jobs easier. I don't think they want to be known for hanging a woman anyway. This will give them a way out.'

★ ★ ★

Jake didn't emerge from his hotel room until nearly noon when the glare of the sun on his window and growing heat within it forced him to rise, sweaty and still trail-weary. He was hungry, but that could wait. He wanted to settle matters with the law. Neither Jake nor Billy Bostwick had been eager to discuss things when Jake trailed into Lewiston well after midnight.

Bostwick, shirtless, wearing a leather jacket, had come outside, lifted Kit Blanchard's head and nodded. That was about all. Bostwick had taken the time to inform Jake that Marshal Sam

Trouffant had passed away.

'I think it's those two desert women that gave him a heart attack,' Bostwick said.

'They were enough to do it,' Jake agreed.

Jake had also learned that Christiana was in her hotel room, being held under guard. The rest of it, he decided could wait until morning.

He had seen the two Fulton brothers riding out of town as he made his way toward the jail. He did not know their names, but knew they had been Hutch Gleason's men. They had ridden with the posse. It seemed that they had had enough.

Billy Bostwick was in his usual position at the marshal's office, boots propped up on the desk. He glanced up to find Jake there without surprise or any other visible emotion.

'Good day, Staggs,' Bostwick said without enthusiasm. 'What brings you around?'

'Just decided to turn myself in,' Jake

replied. Bostwick drew a hand across his face and shook his head.

'What'd you do now?' the deputy asked.

'Stole another horse,' Jake said. He seemed to be causing Bostwick some discomfort.

'Did you, now?'

'The dun I was riding — it belongs to the man you had locked up here,' Jake confessed.

'I know it,' Bostwick said, his eyes growing intolerant. 'Will Sizemore. He told me that he loaned it to you, that that was what he and you were talking about yesterday. Look, Staggs, I appreciate that you think of yourself as a law-abiding citizen and all, but you've got to learn to restrain yourself.'

'I took the dun.'

'You're the only one accusing yourself of taking that horse. And you're known around here for making false confessions. Forget it, will you?' Bostwick reached into the bottom drawer of his desk, withdrew a wide, slender envelope and slid it across toward Jake.

'What's this?'

'Why, the reward money. It's a bank draft covering the bounties on Lemon Jack Baker, River Tremaine and Eduardo Blanco. It totals fifteen hundred dollars; five hundred on Blanco, a thousand on the other two combined. Once they disburse the five thousand for Kit Blanchard, you'll be set pretty good, Staggs.'

'I don't want it,' Jake said.

'Of course you do. Anyone would,' Billy Bostwick said. 'You're thinking that it was that woman, Sarah Worthy who wanted to go after it, well she's gone now, isn't she? The money's been disbursed. It can't be sent back. I can't take it; it would be like I had found some scheme to line my own pockets. Besides,' he said after a pause, 'there's no denying that you're the man that did the shooting.'

'No,' Jake said thoughtfully. 'There's no denying that.'

Worthy had pled with Jake not to get

him involved in the killing of Kit Blanchard. 'I've enough money to get by on,' he had said. 'I don't need any reward. I don't want to show my face in Lewiston. I don't care to talk to the law. They might decide to take me in on charges that I was harboring the gang. You keep whatever cash might be on Kit's head, Jake. It's yours.'

'I guess it's mine,' Jake said to Bostwick, and he picked up the envelope, folded it and stuffed it into his shirt pocket.

'Personally,' Bostwick said rising from his chair now, his face severe. 'I think that this might be a good time for you to make the most of this opportunity and leave Lewiston. The truth is, you're more trouble than you're worth. Although we will miss Cathy.'

Cathy? What did she have to do with this?

Just about everything, Jake realized as he exited the office and stood on the plankwalk, peering up the dusty street through the white glare of day. She had wanted to go somewhere, away from the dry heat and wild winds of the desert, to try to just live decently somewhere else. Wasn't that what she had said? What if he were to walk into that restaurant right now and tell her to go home and pack up? What would she say?

Hesitantly, he started that way and nearly walked into Will Sizemore. Jake stiffened and his hand hovered near his pistol. The craggy old outlaw smiled.

'You won't be needing that, Staggs. I told you that we were sitting on the opposite side of the table, but that was when Kit was alive. A lot of men hated Kit, but I owed him some favors. Now that he's gone, it's over.'

'You told the deputy that you let me borrow your horse.'

'Yes I did,' Sizemore replied, removing his hat to run his hand across his bald head. 'I was still in jail last night when the stablehand came in to report that he thought a man had acted kind of suspicious — you — when he asked for the dun. And that you had said that you were a deputy marshal. So I told Bostwick that was just what you and me had been talking about: you wanted to borrow my horse. I knew it didn't matter anymore: Kit would be dead or he would shoot you. Either way, I figured to get my horse back sooner or later. Besides, the dun didn't cost me nothin',' the horse thief said with a wink.

'What did happen to Kit?' Will Sizemore wanted to know. 'I can't imagine you beating him in a fair fight.'

'Worthy shot him,' Jake said. 'He blamed Kit for what had happened to the girls.'

'I see,' Sizemore said. 'That makes more sense. No offense, Jake, but it's a good thing the old man was there. Kit Blanchard would have shot you to ribbons. Well, you're free and clear now, aren't you?'

'Except for that buckskin horse of mine,' Jake said gloomily.

'The one with the Broken T brand?' Sizemore asked with a grin. 'Why, brother, do you know how many ways there are to change that brand with a hot cinch ring?'

'No, I've never been in that business, and I don't intend to start learning now.'

Sizemore nodded, planted his hat again and then said, 'Well then, you darned fool, why don't you just take the simple way out?' At Jake's puzzled look, the old outlaw went on. 'I was in jail still when the reward money was delivered. Boy, use common sense! You've got enough money to pay for that horse ten times over. Write to the man who owned it. Ask him would he like you to ship it to him, or would he take cash money for it. Odds are he'll take the money.'

Jake stood there for a moment, stunned at his own stupidity. Well, he thought, sometimes it takes someone on the outside of a problem to solve it.

'I believe I'll do that. Today.'

'Do that. You deserve to start fresh.'

'What about you, Will?'

'I only know one way to live, Staggs. I think I'll wander back over to the gulch and see if any of the other boys have come around.'

'I don't think Worthy will stand for it again.'

'Well, then,' Sizemore shrugged, 'we'll find us a new place. Smuggler's Gulch never brought any of us any luck anyhow, did it?'

No, no it hadn't, Jake reflected as he walked on towards the restaurant. Or maybe it had, in a strange convoluted way. He was now free of his concerns and had money in his pocket. And maybe, with just the smallest bit of luck, had Cathy to start a new life with.

It was early evening before they had gotten all of Cathy's possessions loaded onto the buckboard. Her friends were still at work, and Jake had offered to wait with her until they came home so that she could tell them goodbye, but she had already said her goodbyes at the restaurant.

'Besides, we should get started,' she

told him. 'We don't want to be on the trail after nightfall.'

She was wearing her yellow dress and a yellow bonnet as Jake helped her to step up onto the buckboard. Her eyes were concerned, determined and doubtful at once.

'It'll be fine, Cathy,' Jake told her. 'I'll make it my business to see that everything is fine for you.'

She smiled then, and held the smile until he had clambered up and taken the reins to the two-horse team. The buckskin was tethered on behind, now apparently frisky enough for a new adventure.

Jake held the team up, looking back at the house. Cathy watched him. 'Jake, what's holding us up?'

'Nothing,' he said with a grin as Chaser darted from the bushes toward the wagon. 'Come on then, you dumb mutt! It's time we were leaving.'

And Jake started the buckboard forward, following the rough trail across the desert, the red dog with the broom of a tail panting happily after them.

Author's Note

Smuggler's Gulch is a real place used in the late 1800s as described in the novel. It is actually located in Southern California, not Arizona, and has recently been the site of modern smuggling, chiefly of drugs and of illegal aliens from Mexico.